A FRENCH KISS OF DEATH

Colonel Romand led so depraved a life that his beautiful widow wept tears of joy at his death, and the village priest called the hunting accident that claimed his life an act of God.

M. Pinaud of the Paris Sûreté called it an act of common murder. And he knew any one of the four men shooting rabbits that tragic morning had a motive to commit it. Woodsman Ulysse Dumont openly hated the man who had seduced his daughter. Salesman David Marbon knew Romand had been his pretty wife's lover. Handsome young Louis Brevin thought death too easy an end for the monster who had debauched his teenaged fiancée. And Dr Justerton, the town physician, felt killing Romand would rid the village of a pestilence.

Spotting the real killer should have been simple for the greatest French detective of them all . . . if only his eyes hadn't been dazzled by the diverting charms of Romand's lovely daughter . . . and if someone didn't kill him first.

Scene of the Crime® Mysteries

Murder Ink® Mysteries

A Scene Of The Crime® Mystery

SLAY ME A SINNER

Pierre Audemars

A DELL BOOK

Published by
Dell Publishing Co., Inc.
1 Dag Hammarskjold Plaza
New York, New York 10017

Dell ® TM 681510, Dell Publishing Co., Inc.

ISBN: 0-440-18191-7

Reprinted by arrangement with Walker and Company

Printed in the United States of America

First Dell printing—July 1983

To
Basil Blowfield
with the author's respect, admiration
and gratitude

A slow song beaten and broken,
As it were from the dust and the dead,
As of spirits athirst unsloken,
As of things unspeakable spoken,
As of tears unendurable shed.

Swinburne: *Tenebrae*

I

In the days when M. Pinaud had come to the richly satisfying evening of his life, he found it far easier to remember certain of his earlier cases than those, far more complicated, which had so recently brought him some measure of justly celebrated fame.

As, for example, the inexplicable death of Colonel Romand of Vallorme, which he knew he would never forget.

According to his chronicler (who is only concerned with the truth) this case was not without a certain interest, and therefore the intensity of recollection and the vividness of memory were both logical and understandable.

But when such observations were made, innocently enough, in his hearing, M. Pinaud would immediately become profoundly depressed and had even been heard to mutter such words as senility and decrepitude, followed by remarks, hurtful enough to one of a sensitive nature, as to how any presumption or bias, however slight, could be nothing but prejudicial to an impartial recording of the truth . . .

To M. le Chef, naturally, this case was nothing more than one of Pinaud's early failures.

To his eternal credit, he never formulated this opinion in actual words. Even in those days he was quick to recognize all the qualities latent in his youngest employee—that single-minded and almost fanatical devotion to duty, that amazing physical strength and endurance, that rapier-like intelligence and that intuitive insight into character and behaviour— qualities which he knew would eventually earn him rightful acclaim as the greatest detective the *Sûreté* had ever known.

M. le Chef realized all this after reading his report. With tact and discretion unusual in a perfectionist—not to mention a considerable amount of difficulty, for this was hardly in his nature—he kept his mouth tightly shut and thought profoundly instead of launching into his usual tirade of condemnation and castigation at an unsolved crime.

One did not discourage the young. One should never reprimand them for their mistakes. How else could they hope to learn—except by making them? One directed their ardour and enthusiasm and guided them into the proper channels.

And then—and then—all that was needed was a little patience. The reputation of the *Sûreté* was bound to reflect the honour and the glory and the eminence of the man who so successfully directed it . . .

*　　*　　*

14

'Go on, then,' M. Pinaud said to his chronicler in one of these moods of depression. 'Go on—since you insist. Tell them about Colonel Romand. I was young then. To me everything was either black or white. There was no such colour as grey. Either a thing was right or else, conversely, it was bound to be wrong. What an insufferable young prig I must have been.

'Everything in my mind was clear-cut and definite. I was being paid to do my duty. Because of my very nature, the acceptance of my microscopic salary bound me morally to an obligation whose fulfilment became a point of honour. I was the representative of the law. It was both my duty and my privilege to enforce it.

'My work was determined by an invariable rule and an inflexible guide. Detailed to investigate any violent and mysterious death, I always asked myself one question: who wanted the person dead, who benefited by the death? The answer to that question nearly always solved the mystery.

'But go on. Tell them. Tell them how that case was the first step in teaching me tolerance and compassion and understanding. Tell them about Father Lafarge. Tell them some of the things he told me.

'I can remember them all. I have never forgotten them. I have never seen him since. He is probably dead by now— even in those days he was a far older man. But he would have been pleased if ever I had found the time to travel down there again and tell him how the seeds his words contained germinated and blossomed and bore flowers and fruit that not even the changing years were able to destroy.

'Perhaps some of your younger readers may learn something. Maybe one or two will benefit. With all my faults, I

15

was always willing to learn. If only one or two of them realize and come to accept the fact that with the passing of the years—which nothing can ever change—they too will become old, like I am now, then all the hours you spend scribbling in that notebook of yours will not have been wasted. They too may feel depressed when they find it so easy to remember what happened years ago and have difficulty in recalling what they had for lunch last Tuesday. Go on, tell them all about it.'

He smiled suddenly, and the hard brooding strength of his features was transformed. There were few secrets between them.

'And try to make it interesting. Try to make people laugh as well as cry. Life is hard enough as it is today—and books are so expensive. Try to give them something of value for their money.'

It really began in the early morning of a glorious autumn day when M. Pinaud was driving back home through a very remote district in the south of France.

He had successfully solved the remarkable case of the perverted landlady of Lucarne and the incredibly revolting things she kept in her refrigerator.

In consequence he had been obliged to spend nearly a week away from home. Married to a young and very lovely wife and the father of two small children, his only desire at the moment was to rejoin his family and relax as soon as possible in the peace and tranquillity of his home.

With this in mind, he waited patiently until all the necessary details and formalities had been completed and then said good-bye courteously to a pathetically grateful local *Préfet*, still shaken and white-faced from his recent acute vomiting, having decided to drive all the way back to Paris through what was left of the night, so that with luck he should be home the following evening early enough to participate in the riotous fun of the children's bath.

This decision should present no difficulties, since M. le Chef—after first peremptorily and categorically refusing, then examining his record sheets with a scorn that changed quickly to disbelief and finally to amazement and admiration—had recently acceded formally and officially to his repeated requests for a new car to replace his worn-out one. All he had to do was to keep awake and drive fast, which was something he enjoyed doing.

And so, after finishing a pot of scalding hot black coffee at an all-night café and a modest number of large brandies— purely for medicinal purposes, in order to dull the sickening memories of that nauseating woman and her incredible perversions after she had poisoned her lodgers—and then two hours' nap behind the wheel in the car-park, he set out on his way home.

The sky lightened and imperceptibly grew grey. The early birds began to sing, in unison and in harmony, the first chorus of the dawn.

The road at that hour was deserted. He drove exceptionally fast, but always carefully, never straining the engine nor forcing it to labour. He could no more ill-treat a piece of machinery as miraculously complicated as an internal combustion engine than he could voluntarily inflict pain on a human being.

For a few seconds, on a straight and clear stretch of road, he raised his eyes to the distant hills and on each gradually encircling side. The road through the plain was climbing imperceptibly towards the pass which almost surmounted them, and close ahead, dark and brooding against the ever-lightening sky, the stark bulk of the enormous church at Vallorme seemed to crush the incredibly old squat flint watch-tower its medieval architects had deemed worthy of incorporating as an integral part of their structure.

For a moment he slowed down, wondering why what he knew was a very small town, hardly more than a village, should have such a majestic church. He wished he had paid more attention in his history class at school. There obviously must be a reason, but he did not know it.

One thing, strangely enough, he did remember from all those hours of supreme boredom, and the thought inexplicably comforted him. This was that strange and always mysterious region where an army of Charles Martel had once routed the Saracens, with the result that many of the broken remnants of Abd-el-Rahman's hordes—knowing full well that capture in these parts was only another word for death—had fled to these surrounding and impenetrable hills. To this day, he knew, one could meet and recognize people in these districts with local names who were sometimes strangely dark and swarthy and passionately intense.

As his speed diminished, the road curved and he caught

a glimpse of a beautiful old house through the trees and bushes of a large, densely wooded and fenced-in copse on his right.

He waited to accelerate again, thinking how wonderful it would be if one day he could own a house like that and live there in peace and happiness with his wife and family.

There his children could grow up healthily in the clean and unpolluted country air. There Germaine his wife could feed the wild birds and keep a horse and a dog and a cat and all the animals she loved so much and spend her spare time taking a joy and a pride in tending the flowers in an old-fashioned garden, instead of having to climb up three flights of stairs after her daily shopping and endure each morning the yelling of children as they ran along the ground floors dragging sticks across the iron railings, each afternoon the wailing, screaming and crying of incorrectly brought-up babies, and each night the hideous cacophony of inebriated morons bawling cheerful good-nights to each other.

His window was half down. From the copse he heard the sound of gunfire—the flat reports of shotguns. Some of the locals economizing on their household bills, no doubt, by adding a few rabbits to their larders. This was the right time of day to find them.

And yet, his thoughts continued, it was strange to hear the frequency and the number of shots. From the size and the grandeur of the house he had seen, and the fact that the copse was extensive enough in depth to bound any garden, one would have thought it to have been private property, and as such the shooting rights restricted to one owner.

The gunfire continued as he followed the boundary of the copse. He passed an open gate, through which he noticed a path, curving and leading back into the copse, parallel to the road, and then decided that it was time to accelerate once more.

Perhaps the owner had been entertaining a house-party and had organized an early-morning shoot as a cure for his guests' hangovers.

In any case it did not matter. It was no concern of his. The only important thing was that he was on his way home to his wife and family, and it was a certain and indisputable fact that idling along dreaming of country houses would in no way aid his progress.

He was barely past the gate when the bonnet of his car dipped sharply and his near-side front tyre blew out with a report that drowned the gunfire.

He reacted swiftly, controlled the swerve, braked and steered the car into a level space on the verge of the road. Then he switched off the engine.

For a moment he sat there, motionless, in a mood of savage depression. This he needed like a hole in his head. Changing the wheel would delay him. Calling at the next garage to have the puncture repaired—since he dared not drive so far without a spare wheel—would delay him even more.

Surely with a new car it was not unreasonable to expect new tyres—they had looked new to him—and one should not have to change wheels after a few months. All he wanted to do was to get home as fast as possible to see his wife and family . . .

Then he sighed philosophically, got out of the car and removed his jacket, which he folded neatly and carefully and placed on the seat. He always wore his one and only suit while investigating a case and on the list in his desk at home for replenishment of the family wardrobe his name, somewhat naturally, came at the very end.

Then he opened the boot, drew on an old pair of gloves and busied himself with the spare wheel, the wheel-brace and the jack.

He was on his knees with his head under the front mudguard, searching vainly for a place to set the base of the jack without having to dig a hole in the road—for this was in the days when cars were designed with front axles—which operation, he gathered, should not really be necessary, or else a shovel would have been included in the tool-kit, when he heard the sound of heavy nailed boots on the road approaching him.

He dropped the jack-handle and with some difficulty crawled out backwards and stood up, wondering in exasperated frustration how long it would take him to clean his trousers and why the highly reputable manufacturers of this rightfully celebrated automobile did not supply a dwarf or a midget with each model to manipulate their jack.

He had been so busy since this new and improved model was delivered that he had not yet found time to devote a quiet and peaceful afternoon to familiarizing himself with everything that was strange on it. He had obviously located and examined the dip-stick to check the engine oil level, but as one did not normally expect a puncture with new tyres, all the rest had been put off.

Now after this first quick and impatient examination it seemed to him that he would be able to jack the car up quite successfully were he amputated at mid-thigh.

Now he was in a mess. He had deliberately chosen this road which led through the higher pass by Vallorme because it saved a considerable distance, which was an important consideration when driving home to one's family in a hurry, but just now he could not help thinking of the main road he had so thoughtlessly abandoned with its steady stream of lorry drivers, any one of whom would gladly have pulled up to help him.

A short thickset figure was walking towards him. He must have come out of the copse by the path through the open gate, since the road ahead had been empty as he knelt to begin his operations with the jack.

He was a man of middle age, burly, and obviously immensely strong. The rolled-up sleeves and open neck of his gaily striped flannel shirt revealed muscular and corded forearms ending in thick and powerful hands and a hairy chest like a barrel. He had a small pug nose, hair cropped short, and ugly and yet oddly appealing features with deep-set humorous eyes.

Under his right arm he carried a heavy-barrelled shotgun and from his left hand dangled lifelessly a brace of large rabbits, their hindlegs split and expertly jointed.

'Ho—ho—ho,' he roared in a voice powerful enough to almost drown another report from within the copse. 'At first when I heard you, I thought some lunatic was trying to shoot rabbits with a rifle, but then I thought again. Puncture I said it would be as I came out on the road and saw you, m'sieu—and puncture it is.'

He slowed his pace as he came nearer, but neither

stopped nor ceased bellowing. With the spare wheel propped up against the running-board and the brace with which he had loosened the wheel-nuts on the deflated wheel beside it, M. Pinaud felt that there was little to be gained by denying his triumphant assertion, but he was given no chance to speak.

'Puncture it must be,' the great voice roared on happily, 'and I, Ulysse Dumont, a man who is seldom wrong, can tell you the cause of it. And what is more, I will share my knowledge with you, since it is your tyre and your puncture.'

There was logic in what he said, and therefore M. Pinaud could not argue. On the other hand, he was not really interested in the cause, and the longer this individual bellowed and wasted his time here the later he would arrive home.

'I do not think that is really necessary—'

But he was wasting his breath in trying to speak.

'Builders' nails. Ten centimetres with large flat heads. They deliver them with trucks in open half-kegs piled up to the brim. The trucks take the corners too fast and some spill out on the floor. Then when they go over a bump some more slide out through the gaps under the tailboard. Some stand upright on their heads. You will find one in your tyre, m'sieu. Want to bet on it?'

By now he had drawn level and passed the car. He did not stop walking but continued towards the town. Like M. Pinaud, he obviously had more important things to do. But with his head over his shoulder, the roar of words continued for a while unabated.

'Name your own figure. You have an honest face and so I trust you. Give your stake to my friend Jean Latour in town when he gives you the nail. He is the finest mechanic

23

in the south-west. You will need a spare to get back—from your number-plate it is a long way.'

He went on walking at the same unhurried pace, and although some faint echoes of that tremendous voice still floated back on the still early morning air, the words were now indistinguishable.

Then he waved the heavy rabbits as if they were feathers in a gesture of farewell, turned his head the right way and disappeared round the next bend in the road.

M. Pinaud smiled wryly as he remembered his theory explaining the number and the frequency of the shots he had heard. This one hardly looked the type to have been a house-guest of the owner of that lovely house.

Anyway, it did not matter. The copse was large enough to accommodate both poachers and shooting-parties, especially if the former kept under cover in the dense foliage. Poaching here was probably an age-old custom in Vallorme.

He was about to get down on his hands and knees again when he saw another man coming out of the path from the copse to the road. He therefore changed his mind and waited erect beside the car until the approaching figure was near.

This was a much younger man, with a short curly growth of beard and a large drooping moustache which together almost completely concealed the lines of his mouth. He was of average height and slim, but inclining to paunchiness around the middle. His eyes, which at his age should have been clear and alert, were veined and bloodshot, pouched and dull and strained.

He, too, cradled professionally a heavy double-barrelled shotgun under his arm, but his other hand was empty. He carried no rabbits.

'I say—have you got a puncture?' he called out as he stopped.

'Yes.'

M. Pinaud's reply was perhaps a little more abrupt than good manners might have dictated, but by now his impatience was mounting as rapidly as a fever.

The young man took a step nearer and eyed the car with undisguised approval. He smiled suddenly and his features were transfigured.

'Hard luck—especially with new tyres. I heard it blow. This is the latest model, isn't it?'

'Yes. Just out.'

'I am a traveller. I have got last year's model—marvellous cars. No hope for a new one until I have done the required mileage.'

'Yes—it is a very fine car.'

M. Pinaud's impatience vanished, his tone changed completely and he too smiled.

'Providence must have sent you, m'sieu,' he continued with great sincerity. 'Perhaps you would be kind enough to tell me whether the manufacturers have supplied me with the right jack, and if so, where and how I put it.'

'Of course.'

The young man laid his shotgun down carefully on the grass bank at the side of the road and came round to the front of the car. Without hesitation he dropped on one knee and peered under the wing, which M. Pinaud had been taught to call a mudguard.

In a matter of seconds he stood up again, brushing the knee of his trousers with one hand.

'Thought so—just like mine. They haven't really changed much on the chassis. Most of the improvements are in the engine. You will see that small projection under and in front of the stub-axle. The flat top of the jack—yes—same as mine—just fits underneath.'

'That is most kind of you,' M. Pinaud told him with great civility and a deep thankfulness. 'I am extremely grateful and much obliged to you.'

'Not at all.'

He turned to pick up his shotgun and then paused and hesitated.

'Would you like any help—'

'No—no—you are very kind—but I can manage. I have changed a few wheels in my life. It was just the jack that bothered me—my last car was of a different make.'

'Good. Then I'll be on my way home.'

He picked up the shotgun, cradled it easily and thrust his other hand into his pocket.

'Please accept my thanks once again,' M. Pinaud said. 'You had no luck with your shooting, then?'

For a second—so briefly that M. Pinaud thought afterwards he might have imagined it—some indefinable emotion seemed to glow in those dull and strained eyes. Then he turned his head and looked back at the path he had just used to leave the copse.

'No. I am afraid I have too much on my mind at the moment. To shoot rabbits successfully one needs concentration. Good-bye.'

He turned and walked away, quite slowly, towards the town.

* * *

The intensive firing had ceased. Now only an occasional shot tore through the peaceful stillness of that lovely sunlit morning.

The dog, a magnificent black retriever, came bounding out of the path on to the side of the road.

He saw M. Pinaud bending over the punctured wheel, removing the loosened nuts with the brace, and without hesitation hurled himself forward to investigate.

Then he saw something far more interesting—the gleaming and shining spare wheel with its immaculate and unused tyre propped up against the running-board. He sniffed at it in an ecstasy of approval, took a pace forward and lifted his leg. Then he turned, wagged his tail and looked up, the beautiful lambent brown eyes pleading intelligently for commendation.

M. Pinaud straightened up and sighed. He was very fond of dogs, and this was undoubtedly one of the most beautiful he had ever seen. But this—this was too much. With regard to his car, he was fanatically fastidious. He would shortly be handling that spare wheel. He had on a pair of old gloves, but even so—

'Nero—Nero—'

A man's voice called from the open gate. Obediently Nero, with a spring of his powerful haunches, leapt off to obey his master's summons.

A young man came down the path and walked towards the car, Nero now following sedately at his heels.

'Well—well,' he called out cheerfully before he drew level, 'I would say that looks like a puncture to me.'

M. Pinaud may be forgiven for thinking, swiftly and perhaps even savagely, that the evidence was surely sufficient to convince not only any normal individual, but even a half-wit or a moron, but he made a great effort, nodded his head civilly, and studied the new arrival with an interest from which he strove to eradicate the bitterness.

He saw a tall young man, lean and fit and handsome, with long black hair and light grey eyes. His mouth was wide and sensitive, with two deep lines of suffering running down to it at each end.

He wore the same kind of clothing as his predecessors—a pullover, old trousers and massive boots, and he too cradled a heavy shotgun under his arm. His morning, however, must have been more successful than the others, since the legs of several rabbits protruded from the open top of an old haversack he wore slung over his other shoulder.

'I see you have done better than the young man with the beard who just came out,' M. Pinaud told him, feeling slightly remorseful at the thoughts which might have prompted him to incivility.

The man laughed, revealing a mouthful of large and excellent white teeth.

'Yes. That would have been David Marbon—he is a rotten shot, anyway. And he has problems. And besides, I have an advantage. I have Nero.'

And as he spoke he stooped down to pat the dog's head.

The pride and affection in his voice as he mentioned the name were somehow strangely and poignantly moving. M. Pinaud would have dearly liked to own such a dog himself, but the demands and exigencies of his exacting and arduous profession left him no time for the love and affection such a magnificent creature deserved.

'Ah yes—Nero—'

In spite of his remorse at his uncharitable thoughts and perhaps because of this envy, M. Pinaud could not help looking pointedly at his spare wheel. At the sound of his name repeated twice, the dog whimpered, softly and eagerly, with joy and anticipation.

The young man followed his gaze. The evidence of Nero's incontinence was unmistakable. The smile vanished, the teeth disappeared. He laid his gun down carefully on the grass verge and dropped the haversack.

'I say—I am so very sorry about that. Let me clean—'

M. Pinaud interrupted him without compunction. He now felt doubly remorseful at the ungracious way in which he was behaving, but all he wanted to do now was to get home as soon as possible to see his wife and children, and that simple and uncomplicated wish seemed to be the one thing a malignant fate was determined to thwart and deny.

'No—no—please—there is no need to bother. After a few kilometres in this dust it will no longer be there. And besides—I have a pair of gloves.'

'But—'

'No—no. I insist.'

'I do really apologize—'

'There is no need. I would be proud if Nero were mine.'

Again at the sound of his name the dog looked up and whimpered, and this time—at what he recognized instantly in this human's voice—a deep responsive rumble from the back of his throat accompanied the sound.

'I am very proud,' the young man replied, and smiled

again. 'Well—at least let me help you to change the wheel.'

'Thank you—it is kind of you to offer—but again that is not necessary. The jack is on, the nuts off, the wheel up ready to be changed, as you can see—just a matter of a few moments. But I appreciate your offer.'

'Very well.'

He picked up his gun and shouldered the haversack.

'You will want to get that repaired before you go on. There is a very good garage in town—Latour is the name. He will oblige you quickly.'

'Thank you. I will call there.'

'Good-bye, then. Come on, Nero.'

He walked on rapidly towards the town, Nero following decorously at his heels, and M. Pinaud bent to remove the punctured tyre.

He tightened the last nut on the spare wheel, lowered and disengaged the jack and replaced it in its clip. Then he tightened all the five nuts once again. He turned the punctured wheel around against the running-board until he saw the flat head of the nail protruding and the ugly gash in the wall of the tyre.

Ulysse Dumont had been justified in his contention that he was a man seldom wrong. It was fortunate, M. Pinaud reflected, that he himself had made no commitments nor mentioned any specific figures with regard to bets on the cause of his puncture—fortunate and even merciful, in view of the salary M. le Chef considered an adequate and satisfying compensation for his labours.

The firing from the copse had finally ceased. Tentatively, the birds began to sing again.

He lifted the punctured wheel to fix it on its bracket and then became aware that yet another man with a shotgun under his arm was standing on the grass verge in front of him.

The voice that accosted him was cultured, concerned and very polite.

'Excuse me—but have you had a puncture, m'sieu?'

For one mad and savage moment he thought of replying in a manner which might ease all his pent-up frustration at these continual and unending interruptions.

'Oh no,' he ought to say, 'Whatever gave you that idea? Sometimes appearances can be deceptive. I happen to be a perfectionist. Every five thousand kilometres, wherever I happen to be, I always make a point of changing all my tyres around, to ensure that each one eventually gets the same wear and the different stress. This naturally gives me the opportunity of picking out all the broken flints and sharp stones before they have a chance to penetrate too deeply into the treads. Moreover, with the wheel off—'

He took a deep breath, tried to control his racing thoughts and addressed himself sternly.

Shut up, Pinaud. Sarcasm is the refuge of small minds. Watch your behaviour, or else you will grow, more quickly than you think, into a cantankerous and peevish old bastard. Answer the man civilly, as he deserves. He means well. They all meant well. The first one was quite right about the nail, the second one helped you with the jack, the third one loves that wonderful dog as he deserves.

31

He pushed the spare wheel on to the bracket-screw and forced himself to smile, looking at the man with interest.

He was tall and powerfully built, with a high and intelligent forehead, receding hair and a mouth whose lips were both full and yet strong. His hands, as he lowered the shotgun on its butt and leaned on the barrels, were beautiful— broad and powerful in the palms with long fingers and tapering narrow nails. He wore an old velveteen shooting-jacket and a pair of the most disreputable trousers M. Pinaud had ever seen.

'Yes,' he replied with equal politeness. 'I had the misfortune to pick up a nail—just when I am in a hurry to get back to Paris.'

'Bad luck.'

'It could have been worse. There might have been two, one each side of the road. I have changed the wheel, and not much time has been lost.'

He gestured towards the gun.

'Have you just come from the copse, m'sieu?'

'Yes. Dr Justeron, at your service. I am fortunate in that my surgery does not open until nine o'clock, and as I am the only doctor in Vallorme I have no competition.'

'My name is Pinaud. I live in Paris. Success in that copse, M'sieu Justeron, seems to depend on the individual. While I have been changing my wheel, two have come out with rabbits and you are the second without any.'

The doctor smiled easily.

'That could be. It is big enough and dense enough for several to shoot at the same time without even seeing each other. I heard the shots and gathered that I was not alone, but I did not see anyone. My excuse is that rabbits do not

normally suffer from a hangover, and therefore their reflexes are rather more rapid and efficient.'

He laughed and swung the heavy gun up easily under
his arm.

'But I only come for the exercise—I am not particularly
fond of rabbit.'

He turned and began to walk on towards the town. Over
his shoulder he called:

'Good-bye, M'sieu Pinaud. I hope you have a good
journey back with no more punctures.'

'Thank you.'

M. Pinaud tightened the locking-nut on the spare wheel,
replaced the brace and the jack in their places, took off his
gloves and put on his jacket.

Then he lit a cigarette. He was ready to go. For a
moment he wondered guiltily whether he should have
offered the doctor a lift as they were both obviously going
to the town. He would almost certainly overtake him. That
would mean more talk and more delay, when all he wanted
to do was to get home. The best thing to do was to drive
by fast and pretend not to see him.

He walked round to the back of the car to check that he
had shut the boot and not left anything lying about. Then
he stopped in astonishment.

Down the path, at a flying run, came the figure of a
young girl. She wore a short and deceptively simple-looking

summer frock, whose skirt rode high above her knees as she ran, and obviously not very much beneath it.

She was astonishingly and breath-takingly beautiful, with dark eyes, a wide and passionate mouth and raven-black shoulder-length hair which streamed out wildly as she ran. And she was clearly frightened, upset and distressed.

He took a few quick steps forward to intercept her and held out his arms.

'Easy now—easy,' he said quietly and gently. 'What is the matter?'

He braced himself as she crashed into him with the impetus of her run and held her firmly around the waist. Then he shifted his hands to her upper arms and supported her while she fought to regain her breath.

'Tell me,' he continued, as casually as if they had been formally introduced in a drawing-room. 'Tell me what happened.'

This one was young, but also she was already sex incarnate. He felt it in the warm soft flesh still pressed hard against his groin, he could sense it slumbering behind the shocked and dilated pupils of her eyes and he could see it plainly in the way she looked him up and down lustfully and appraisingly, in spite of her obvious shock and terror, with her parted lips accentuating her quick and excited breathing.

A memory of his headmaster suddenly flashed through his mind as he waited for her to speak.

He had been summoned for the dreaded interview in the celebrated study a few days before he left the senior form for good. He saw again the spare and angular figure, the deeply lined and compassionate features beneath the mane of snow-white hair as clearly and vividly as if it had been yesterday.

He had not known at the time that the previous visitor in that study had been a complaining and almost apoplectic parent of a pupil at the affiliated girls' school nearby, somewhat justifiably outraged at the behaviour of his young daughter, and yet coherent enough to mention the offending and licentious pupil in the senior form by name.

Also he had not known that the headmaster had soothed and calmed the angry parent, handling him with tact and consideration but steadfastly refusing to allocate more blame to his one named pupil than to the delinquent daughter and the other seventeen lustful members of his senior form. This he had only learnt later.

He heard once again the deep and resonant voice enunciating each word and rounded period with exquisite and pedantic diction.

'Ah yes—Pinaud. You are young and strong and intelligent, and—if one is to believe the infuriated father I have just interviewed—the possessor of a quite exceptional virility. The world should be at your feet. But try to reflect on what that visiting Anglican bishop told you in his talk to school-leavers last week. About leading a godly, sober and righteous life. Find the true glory of your strength, Pinaud, not only in fulfilling your manifold desires, but in controlling them.'

He paused for a moment, and the look in his eyes had seemed to pierce like a sword.

'That is all I have to say. You know very well what I am talking about. I wish you good fortune and Godspeed.'

The memory and the images vanished and once again he was alone with this girl.

35

'My father—' she gasped. 'There has been a dreadful accident. He is dead—in the copse. His head—it is awful—horrible—'

She shuddered and quivered and he tightened his grasp with gentle strength in sympathy. Words were not necessary. They could mean nothing. The very acceptance of his silence seemed to surge in understanding between them.

And then, sweetly and suddenly, the birds began to sing together—it seemed from every scrub and bush and tree—until the whole world seemed filled with the sound and the beauty of their singing, and even the light of the sun seemed to throb and quiver and resound, as if striving to dominate that exquisite harmony, as if seeking to shine through that lilting melody, as if vibrating in concord with the magic of their song.

Far above his head a lark quivered and fluttered against the soft azure depths of the sky, as faintly and yet unmistakably his high call floated down to earth, a sword in that sheath of sound, a spear in the velvet softness of their singing, a chord—high and clear and piercing sweet—in that glorious threnody of song . . .

2

He released his grip and stepped back.

'Take me there,' he told her quietly. 'Show me where he is. You need not look again.'

Without a word she turned and began to walk back up the path. In three strides he was beside her. She seemed calmer now and when she spoke her voice was almost normal.

'Mother found him. She sent me out here to stop the first motorist and ask him to tell the police. Our telephone is not working. There is—there is no need for a doctor.'

'I will go myself—as soon as I have seen him,' he told her.

The path seemed to be running parallel with the road. In a moment she turned off to follow a narrow track, which led over twisted and tangled roots towards the house. He followed closely behind her.

Now the young trees were taller and denser, their topmost branches mingling inextricably as they fought to seek the light. Shrubs, bushes and prolific undergrowth made almost impenetrable banks on either side of the track.

Here in the heart of the copse were coolness and shade, silence and peace. Even the singing of the birds seemed muted and forlorn, as if only its echoes could filter through from another world.

The track twisted and turned, rose and climbed, dipped and fell. After a sharp turn, at the foot of a descending slope, he saw the body lying full-length face downward.

The girl stopped suddenly and began to shiver again.

'There is no need to wait,' he told her gently. 'You go on up to the house. I will come to see your mother in a moment.'

Then his voice changed.

'Where is the gun?'

'I—I took it inside—to Mother. On my way out, when I saw him lying there, I went to look, although she told me not to. And I saw it. I was frightened. I thought someone else might get hurt. One barrel was still loaded—'

'You should not have done that,' he told her.

'Why not?'

He did not answer, but walked on towards the body, and knelt on one knee beside it.

'Where was the gun?' he asked.

She had followed him. Now she pointed.

'Just about there—behind him. You can see where the long grass is still flattened.'

'Good. You go on now.'

'Very well. Follow this track and you will come out into our garden.'

'Thank you.'

He waited until she had gone and then, fighting to control his sickness, he placed one hand beneath the man's chin, then turned and lifted what was left of his head.

In the long years that were to pass he became inured and hardened to such dreadful sights. In those days it was all he could do not to vomit. The muzzle of the barrel must have been quite close; the back and top of the man's head were shattered to a pulp.

He forced himself to study and memorize the features. The forehead, which had escaped injury, was high and intellectual, in strange contrast to the pouched and hooded eyes, glazed and staring now in death, and the loose and sensual mouth.

It was an evil and depraved face, even in the peaceful majesty of death, and he withdrew his hand with a feeling of wonder. How could such a type ever have fathered this lovely girl?

Then his mind began to reason—swiftly, logically and competently. It could well have been an accident.

He would have been carrying the shotgun under his arm, both barrels loaded, the safety-catch off, ready to swing up, aim and fire at the sight of the first rabbit. Coming down that narrow and twisting slope, his foot might have caught in one of the many protruding roots, causing him to trip and overbalance. Walking forward and downhill, he would inevitably have fallen forward, throwing out his hands instinctively to break his fall and save his face. The gun under his arm would have dropped. A branch or a root might have struck the trigger a second before he was prone—the gun would have fallen more quickly because of its weight than a man staggering to retain his balance—

39

with its barrel in line with the back of his head. There had been a bruise on his forehead consistent with a fall.

It could have been an accident.

But he thought that the odds were about a million to one against so many conjectures, assumptions and probabilities all happening together at the same time. It was far more likely and even more probable that there could be a simpler, quite logical and entirely different explanation . . .

He straightened up, brushed the knee of his trousers absent-mindedly and walked very slowly to where the impression of the shotgun was still discernible on the turf and leaves behind the body, his mind still reasoning coolly and calmly and logically.

Again he knelt down, this time to examine the dense growth of brushes and young trees on either side of the track. Its surface was uneven with a profusion of tangled and half-projecting roots.

A man could easily trip and stumble over them. But if he was her father then he lived here and owned this copse. In that case he would know every path and track like the back of his hand.

He continued to look, slowly and thoroughly and painstakingly. And because he knew for what he was looking he found it easily.

At one place, across the track in a straight line, the pattern of leaves, dead twigs and weeds had been very slightly disturbed. He stood up and with infinite care he examined all the trunks of the young trees nearby, forcing his way through the almost impenetrable thicket of young bushes and shrubs which grew everywhere between.

On the left he found nothing. On the right, on the far side of a slender ash tree, he noticed a slight abrasion on the bark at the base of its trunk. If an old and discoloured cord or rope had been tied around it, carefully covered and concealed across the track, and then the other end suddenly jerked up in front of the man's foot by someone who would have been completely invisible behind the bushes on the other side of the track, then his fall would have been inevitable and explicable.

And in that case the very unlikely supposition that his gun fired the fatal shot with such accurate and split-second timing as to hit the back of his head exactly when it crossed the line of fire need no longer be entertained.

It was not necessarily his own gun that had killed him. Shrubs and bushes that would conceal a person could easily hide a gun. All the shotguns he had seen that morning had been of the same bore and calibre. And even if it had, another shot from the dead man's gun, to discharge one barrel, would only have been another one of many. And as such unnoticed. Fingerprints could have been wiped off, and the owner's superimposed. Now that two women had handled it, nothing could ever be proved.

He looked down ruefully at what the thorns and sharp ends of broken branches had done to his one and only suit, but as he walked on up the track towards the house there were so many other thoughts in his mind that dismay simply had no place.

*   *   *

To emerge from the almost cathedral-like gloom of the copse into the brilliant sunshine was as if entering another world.

The house, he saw as he came through a gap on to a well-kept lawn, was large and old and beautifully maintained, but his impression was only fleeting and vague, because all his attention was focussed on the figure of the priest who was now crossing the lawn to meet him.

He wore the habitual *soutane* and wide belt and carried his broad-brimmed hat under one arm.

His hair was iron-grey, his features lined with suffering, his mouth wide and strong and yet at the same time tender and sensitive. And in his deep-set eyes there was an infinite understanding, sympathy and compassion. He reminded M. Pinaud of his old headmaster.

But this one held his head with a pride that made it seem as if it wore a crown. Here, quite unconsciously and perhaps therefore all the more compellingly, was a radiation of the authority of nearly two thousand years of power and domination.

Here was a living manifestation of that spiritual strength which had sent an Emperor to kneel in penitence in the snows of Canossa and the Crusaders to die of sunstroke in their chain-mail within the walls of Jerusalem, that had humbled and taught and inspired the Christian world since the first stone of St Peter's was laid in Rome.

'I give you good morning and the blessing of God,' he said as both men stopped, confronting each other. He raised his hand and made the sign of the Cross. His voice was resonant and strong, and seemed in a strange and indefinable way to carry in its undertones something of that majestic and dominant power he represented.

M. Pinaud bowed his head at the blessing.

'Thank you, Father,' he replied quietly.

'Claudine has just come in and told us that you have been most helpful and kind. I came out myself to thank you. This tragic accident—'

He allowed his resonant voice to die without finishing the sentence but the dark and deep-set eyes never faltered in their intense and penetrating stare.

M. Pinaud's thoughts were swift and chaotic. This one represented the spiritual power; he, for the moment, by virtue of his profession and his appointment, the temporal power. The priest had referred to it as a tragic accident. M. Pinaud knew and believed that if he could get his own way he would shortly be investigating a case of murder. And they were both thinking about the same thing—a dead body lying in the copse behind him. But there seemed to be no point in discussing the matter here and now. He had so many other things to do.

'I tried to help,' he said simply. 'To do what I could. She was naturally very upset.'

'Of course. Although he was not her natural parent but her stepfather. Her mother married recently, after the death of her husband. May I say how pleased I was to hear what you just said. So few people today will accept the responsibility of helping others. It is one of my duties, naturally.

43

Perhaps I am prejudiced. This is a very small town. We all know each other. Most of us worship in the same church. Mme Romand is a woman who needs both sympathy and love. I do what I can. I visit her often. You intend to see her now, m'sieu? Claudine told us you said that you would come to the house.'

'Yes. I would like to have a few details before I report the death to the police.'

'She is already expecting you—'

For a moment there was a silence as he hesitated. This seemed sufficiently incompatible with what M. Pinaud had been able to gather of his character that he looked at him with some curiosity. The hesitation did not last long.

'This tragic accident—I did not finish just now. Perhaps you wondered why. I began to think. The ways of God are indeed mysterious and sometimes difficult to understand.'

'What do you mean, Father?'

M. Pinaud's voice was expressionless. There was no hesitation in the reply.

'This was a man—I trust I will be forgiven for saying so—who is far better dead.'

'Why?'

The deep-set eyes met his own frankly.

'I know that I should not condemn a fellow-man, and I shall pray for the forgiveness of my sin. But Colonel Hector Romand was an evil and depraved character—a debauched and lecherous swine. The world—and particularly this lovely and unspoilt corner of it—is a cleaner and better place without him.'

M. Pinaud did not answer. The silence seemed to surge back from between them, as if stricken at the implications of what the priest had said. Then, tentatively, now that their voices had ceased, one or two birds began to sing from under the eaves of the roof and the spell was broken.

'May I have your name, m'sieu?'

The resonant voice, which a moment ago had trembled with a passionate intensity of conviction, was now completely different—quiet, courteous and somehow entirely impersonal.

'Pinaud, Father. I live in Paris.'

'Thank you. I am Father Lafarge. Please come with me, M'sieu Pinaud. I will take you to Mme Romand. The front door is the other side—the drive leads to the road further on.'

They walked together in silence to the front of the house.

The priest indicated the white-panelled front door, which was closed, with a wave of his right hand, and then held it out in front of him.

'May I say *au revoir,* M'sieu Pinaud? Try to come to see me, if you can spare a few moments when you have finished. The church is on the top of the hill.'

M. Pinaud took his hand. Its clasp was firm and strong.

'Thank you, Father.'

He watched the priest put on his broad-brimmed hat and walk away down the drive. Then he lifted the tongue of the massive wrought-iron knocker and announced his presence to Mme Romand.

*   *   *

She was surprisingly young to have had a teenage daughter, and he realized now from whom the girl had inherited her astonishing beauty.

Only here, in the features of this woman confronting him, that same loveliness, so fresh and appealing with youth, was but a shadow—only a memory left by sorrow and pain and suffering. The same dark eyes were swollen by countless tears, the same dark hair pulled back carelessly and tied with a ribbon.

She wore a pale blue linen dress with a white collar and cuffs, and a narrow dark blue belt almost covered with loose white rings, which off-set her dark and almost swarthy complexion to perfection.

With an obvious effort she forced a smile as she opened the door wide.

'Good morning—do please come inside.'

'Thank you.'

There was no porch, no hall. He stepped over a beautiful Afghan rug straight into a vast room, with massive beams supporting what must have been most of the weight of the upper floors, with an immense open fireplace at the far end.

All the furnishings—oak chairs and table, sideboard, bookcases and armchairs—were obviously old and worn and yet in impeccable taste, the wine-coloured floral pattern of the curtains a perfect foil for the white plastered walls and black oiled beams.

'Please sit down, m'sieu—can I offer you something to drink?'

'No, thank you, madame. I think I should get on as soon as possible—'

46

'Of course. But I do not even know your name—'

'Pinaud, madame. I live in Paris. I was on my way there when I had a puncture outside your copse and your daughter came running to tell me what had happened. May I say how sorry I am to—'

She looked at him with a strange and direct intensity as she interrupted.

'You are kind and helpful, M'sieu Pinaud, and I am the first to appreciate it. Claudine has already told me what a comfort and a blessing you were to her. Death is always terrifying to the young. But please do not waste your sympathy on me. I have lived with my grief for a long time—I told Father Lafarge just now that I can feel and suffer no more. To me this is a merciful release.'

She paused, nervously twisting her hands together. He did not say anything, but his silence was somehow more understanding and compassionate than any words could have been.

'I married him only to give Claudine a home. This house—in which my family have lived since it was built— costs a fortune to maintain. I just could not afford it. That was the biggest mistake I ever made in my life. He was an evil man. In this quiet and lovely part of the world he taught us all the meaning of hate.'

There was a long moment of silence, which to him seemed somehow almost terrifying in its implications. This was the second time in a few moments that he had heard the same opinion of the dead man. What about the others, who had all been in the copse with him at the same time? Did they feel the same? Here was no accident, but a murder, he was convinced. And before he had even started

47

to investigate, two independent witnesses had confirmed any number of motives.

She had closed her eyes as she finished speaking, and without their animation and vivacity her features appeared even more lined and tragic, older and sadder, used and ravaged and worn . . .

Then she opened them, and the tears glistened unshed in their depths as she tried bravely to smile.

'But all this can be of no interest to you, M'sieu Pinaud. Please forgive me. If you would be kind enough to call at the police-station and tell Inspector Frey what has happened I shall be very grateful. If you follow the drive from this front door you will rejoin the road. Turn right and you will come to your car. Claudine told me where she found you.'

'Of course. I am leaving now. May I just ask you two questions, madame?'

'Naturally.'

'Was your husband in the habit of going out like this— so early in the morning?'

'Oh yes. He was very fond of rabbit, and this is the best time to catch them. He went nearly every morning, if the weather was fine. Mind you, he did not go far, nor stay long. He usually kept to the upper tracks nearest to the house. The copse belongs to the estate, but there has been a right of way through it since the Middle Ages. In consequence quite a number of local people come here for the same reason. If we objected, we could do nothing. We do not mind. There is enough for all. If you were busy changing a wheel after your puncture, you must have heard all the shooting this morning?'

'Yes, I heard it. And what did you do with the shotgun, madame? I understand that your daughter—'

For a second her eyes seemed to glow with what might have been defiance as she interrupted him.

'Yes—she brought it in to me. I told her not to look, but she must have gone just the same. She is young, as you saw, and wilful, and she was terrified and very upset. I had to send her up to bed and give her a sedative. She thought that someone else might get hurt—the safety-catch was off and one barrel still loaded. I told her she was quite right. Why do you ask?'

He shrugged.

'I understand that in a case of violent death the police always prefer to handle the weapon first themselves.'

'You mean—for fingerprints?'

'Yes.'

'I never thought about that. Mind you, I was not exactly calm myself at the time. But I should not think for a moment that Inspector Frey will worry. There can only have been three sets on it—his and hers and mine—even if we had left it there.'

'I see. What did you do with it?'

She met his regard calmly.

'This is gun country, M'sieu Pinaud. Guns are not dangerous if they are handled correctly. I did what I was taught to do by my father. I unloaded the one barrel, cleaned the other with a pull-through and put the gun back on the rack in the gun-room.'

He smiled at her, and the hard strong lines of his features were transfigured.

'From your point of view, madame,' he told her, 'that

was obviously the only thing to do. I will go to the police-station now.'

He held out his hand and took hers in a firm clasp.

'Good-bye, Mme Romand. I am sorry that we should have met in such—'

She disengaged her hand and held it up to interrupt him.

'No. Do not be sorry, M'sieu Pinaud. Do not waste your sympathy. I am grateful for your help. But remember that I am glad and thankful that he is dead.'

3

Vallorme was a small town, grouped mainly on either side
of a very wide main street, which at the far end dipped to
bridge the foaming green and white river before climbing
again to the massive church on the crest of the hill.

M. Pinaud pulled off the road and drove his car straight
into the forecourt of the garage. This must be the estab-
lishment of Jean Latour, he concluded without very much
intensive thought, since it appeared to be the only garage
and the one petrol pump in the town.

A man hurried quickly out of the open shed at the back,
wiping his black and greasy hands on a cloth. Astonishingly, his white overalls and shirt were beautifully clean, as
was his freshly shaven face. M. Pinaud got out.

'You must be M'sieu Latour,' he said.

'That is right.'

The man smiled, showing a great number of very white
teeth. He had a bold and humorous face.

'But—'

'According to your friend, Ulysse Dumont, who advised me to come here, I have a builders' nail in my tyre—'

The smile became a hearty laugh.

'There's a type for you. He got one once in the tyre of his wheelbarrow when he had an enormous load of wood—and he has never forgotten it.'

'He was quite right. I saw it when I changed the wheel. Can you mend it for me now?'

'Of course, m'sieu. Any friend of Dumont is a friend of mine. Can you give me about an hour?'

'Yes. That will be fine. Now I have three telephone-calls to make—one to your police-station here and two long-distance calls to Paris. I will pay for them all, naturally. May I—'

Latour glanced at his number-plate and interrupted him, waving his hand.

'For the police-station, m'sieu, I suggest you use this one in the call-box here. My sweetheart Yvonne will put you through at once—that always has priority. For your Paris calls, please use the telephone in my office inside—through that door. They will take her a little longer, I know, but at least you can shut the door and be private.'

'Thank you.'

M. Pinaud smiled at him with approval. This was a good type, and sympathetic. He was now busily engaged in removing the remaining oil and grease from his hands with a clean cloth in a half-basin of petrol before touching the spare wheel on this immaculate and gleaming new car. He therefore deserved a lavish tip, which he would certainly receive, regardless of whether M. le Chef passed or deleted it on the week's expense-sheet.

Then Pinaud lit a cigarette and walked towards the call-box.

'Vallorme police-station. Good morning.'

'Good morning to you. I would like to speak to Inspector Frey.'

'Your business, please.'

'I wish to report a fatal accident.'

'You can report it to me.'

'I know I can. But Mme Romand asked me to report it to the inspector. Besides, I would like to talk to him.'

'I see. Your name, m'sieu?'

'My name is Pinaud. But that will mean nothing to him. I live in Paris. I was just passing through.'

'Hold on a moment.'

He held on for considerably more than a moment. He lit another cigarette with one hand.

'Frey here.'

The other voice had been bored and without interest. Perhaps understandably. Manning a police-station day and night in shifts in a town like this could hardly have been as exciting as in one behind the Gare de Lyon or near the docks in Marseilles. But this voice was alert and vital. With this one he did not have to waste time.

'There has been a fatal accident in the copse behind his house. A Colonel Romand.'

'He is dead?'

'Yes.'

'How?'

'He must have tripped over a root or something and his shotgun went off behind him as he fell.'

At this stage there was no point in saying anything more. This was a public telephone, and the door of the box did not shut. And Jean Latour was making a big business of cleaning his hands quite near him and obviously listening as hard as he could.

'His wife asked me to report it,' he continued. 'Would you send someone to remove the body as soon as possible—naturally she does not like to leave it—'

'When did this happen?' the quick hard voice interrupted him.

'Impossible to say exactly. I was changing a wheel on the road outside for about an hour, and firing was going on in the copse practically all the time. Three or four people came out and spoke to me. They had been after rabbits. The actual shot that killed him might have been any one of the reports I heard during that hour. Can you send one of your men, Inspector Frey, to collect the body?'

'Why?'

'Because I would like to come along to see you shortly, after I have made another telephone-call.'

'Any special reason?'

'Yes. But I would prefer to explain that to you in your office.'

For a long moment there was silence.

'I see what you mean. Very well. I will send the ambulance now and expect you shortly. Good-bye.'

M. Pinaud replaced the receiver thoughtfully. There

were undercurrents of emotion here that he did not understand.

It was characteristic of him that he had made his appointment with the inspector before knowing the outcome of his next call to M. le Chef. In those days he had not worked for him for very long, but long enough to realize that he was not what one would call an easy character.

On the other hand, he himself was young and firmly convinced that one day he was going to be the greatest detective in France. His self-confidence was unbounded, his conviction in his own capabilities complete.

'Excuse me, m'sieu—'

Latour stood at his elbow, with a wheel-brace under his arm.

'But I could not help overhearing—that door does not shut—did you say that Colonel Romand was dead?'

'Yes.'

Latour smiled happily, took out a battered tin from his pocket and offered him a cigarette rolled around a coarse and jet-black tobacco.

'Good riddance,' he continued, leaning forward to accept a light. 'Good riddance to bad rubbish. And there are quite a number of others in this town who will agree with what I say.'

'What do you mean by that?' M. Pinaud asked him, with some difficulty, between spasms of violent coughing. This was more like inserting his head inside an incinerator than smoking a cigarette.

'Glad you like it,' said Latour cheerfully. 'Nothing like good strong tobacco for cleaning out the lungs. These come from Algeria. I have them sent over every month. I served there in the war and made some friends.'

M. Pinaud looked at him thoughtfully. He had asked a question and the answer had been about tobacco. He decided to ask it again.

'Why did you say that—about Colonel Romand?'

Latour blew out a cloud of acrid blue smoke.

'Because he was a swine and a sod and a shit and a—'

He thought of several other words which were no longer alliterative but are not normally used in conversation with strange clients, and muttered them all very rapidly under his breath. Then he continued to speak with even more eloquence, by now warming to his subject with considerable enthusiasm.

'Only in the Army could he have attained the rank of colonel. I am surprised that of all the men in his regiment no one had the guts to shoot him. Each man, after all, was issued with a gun. I always used to service his car for him. There is no need to go into details, but the things I have found behind the back seat and on the floor under the front ones you would never believe. They confirm what others have told me about him. There are several in this town who had good reason to kill him. Now they will all be truly thankful that the task has been done for them by divine Providence.'

Here he crossed himself reverently and devoutly. Then he threw away his cigarette and took hold of the brace with one large and powerful hand.

'Well—I must get on with your puncture now. Through that door to my office, m'sieu—help yourself.'

* * *

'Do you realize, Pinaud, what time it is?'

'Why—yes, m'sieu. My watch keeps excellent—'

'It may interest you to know that I was in bed and fast asleep until this confounded telephone woke me up with its infernal and unending ringing.'

M. Pinaud sighed inwardly, taking great care not to make the slightest sound. This explained the delay.

His gaze lifted to the wall opposite, where above the plain deal desk a large coloured calendar depicted the full-length photograph of a very lovely Eurasian girl, young and slim and stark naked, shielding but in no way concealing her private parts with one hand and smiling cheerfully as she pointed over her shoulder with the other to where a grass hut stood on a beach of golden sand. In the background glittered an impossibly blue and silver sea.

Sheer association of ideas made him remember snatches of idle headquarters gossip.

At one certain and unvarying time every autumn, the aristocratic wife of M. le Chef always paid a ceremonial visit to her father, the retired admiral, at his country estate. It was rumoured that M. le Chef, maintaining persistently that a man of his position and eminence should never have to be bothered or frustrated with the menial household tasks inherent in living alone, had always successfully solved his problems by engaging a series of young, attractive and willing local girls to ensure that his home continued to function efficiently.

The date, some considerable way below the Eurasian girl's hand, confirmed that this was definitely not the time of year to expect his exalted superior to evince any marked enthusiasm for early-morning telephone-calls . . .

'I am very sorry to have disturbed you, m'sieu,' he said

with great respect and civility, 'but I am convinced that this is a case of murder.'

'What is? What the devil are you talking about?'

Briefly and concisely M. Pinaud recounted the basic details of what had happened in the copse that morning. For once M. le Chef listened without interrupting.

'Where are you now, Pinaud?'

'In the town. Vallorme.'

'Ah yes—you were on your way back from Lucarne, were you not?'

'Yes, m'sieu.'

'But no one expected you before tomorrow.'

'I decided to drive through the night so that I could get home earlier.'

'You must have driven like a lunatic. And now all the hours that you have gained by risking your neck you propose to throw away?'

'This is murder, m'sieu—I am positive,' M. Pinaud told him for the second time.

'I wish all my young men had your enthusiasm, Pinaud. Provided you do not weaken, or fall by the wayside, you will go far.'

'Thank you, m'sieu.'

'Have you telephoned your wife?'

'Not yet, m'sieu. I will do so. As soon as we have finished.'

'You are quite sure that I will agree to this?'

'Of course, m'sieu.'

For a moment there was silence. Then he heard the words he had expected.

'What do you want me to do?'

'Thank you, m'sieu. Telephone Inspector Frey here.

58

Vallorme 148. Organize our collaboration and make him understand that I have your full authority. Tell him you will put written confirmation in the post. These country types swear by the written word. I am going to see him shortly, so I would be grateful if you would do this as soon as I hang up.'

'Very well, Pinaud. Consider it done. You are quite sure it was not an accident?'

'Quite sure. It is so unlikely as to be practically impossible. Besides, I found evidence of the rope that must have been used to trip him—'

'Evidence is not proof, Pinaud. You will need proof. To convict a murderer you must have proof.'

'I know. But that is my problem, m'sieu, not yours. I will find the proof.'

'I am sure you will. I have every confidence in you, Pinaud. My regards to your charming wife. Keep in touch.'

'Thank you, m'sieu. And thank you for your help.'

'Not at all. You certainly deserve it, after what you did at Lucarne. Good-bye for now.'

'Good-bye, m'sieu.'

He lit another cigarette, but before he telephoned his wife he stood up from the chair and turned the calendar so that the photograph faced the wall.

It was all very well for his revered and respected headmaster to eulogize on controlling one's desires, but the sight of that young and lovely girl's pudenda, clearly visible between her spreading fingers, filled him with an almost ungovernable lust.

This was an incontrovertible fact, which his mind, so practical in some ways, so idealistic in others, accepted without question. He was young and healthy and—mentally reviewing his life dispassionately from the age of approximately thirteen onwards—clearly over-sexed.

Such a frame of mind hardly provided a fitting or suitable background for a conversation with his wife Germaine, whom he loved very dearly and with an overwhelming and characteristic intensity, nor, did he feel, would it be in any way conducive to the eloquence necessary to inspire the right note of anxiety, despair and longing expected from a young and ardent husband absent for the fifth night in succession from his marital bed . . .

Then he asked the operator for his home number.

Now his chronicler (who is concerned only with the truth) has no record of the conversation which ensued, since in our hero's notes on this remarkable case the only information was one brief entry: 'telephoned G. to tell her would be delayed.'

But having been in such close contact with this eminent man all his life, and having been privileged to read the charming and moving inscription which had been written in her silver-wedding gift quite recently, he is firmly convinced that in spite of all these distractions, side-issues and conjectures, their conversation together must have been characteristically happy and completely satisfactory.

M. Pinaud's nature was far too complicated for him to be able to close his mind into insulated compartments, each one concentrating only on the matter immediately in hand. His thoughts were nearly always confused and complex, radiating outwards and yet at the same time—created spontaneously by some chance word or action—reflecting inwardly in that miraculous intermingling which is the wonder of thought.

He still wanted to get home as much—if not more—than ever, to see her and be with her, to hear the sound of her voice and glory in the love that gave the light to her eyes, to rejoice with humility and thankfulness in the exhausting and yet completely satisfying company of his young children . . .

All these things—to one so close to him spiritually, mentally and physically—must have been clearly apparent to her in the very tone of his voice.

But always to him his duty came first. Perhaps more so then, when he was so much younger, than in later years. Not only was he conscientious to a fault, but because the salary he was paid enabled him to support a wife and family—not in luxury—but at least in circumstances adequate enough for a very great happiness. Therefore to him it became an obligation—more, a point of honour—to earn it fairly and honestly, because of the importance of what it represented. And so there could be no hesitation. He would have to stay in Vallorme.

The decision, he felt, had really very little to do with him. It had already been made.

He bought petrol until his tank was full, paid Latour for the puncture and the telephone-calls and—after having inspected with approval the still immaculate condition of his beautiful new car—added a generous tip.

'Thank you, m'sieu. Thank you very much indeed. I have checked and pumped all the tyres. You will find the Crown Hotel over the bridge and up the hill. Mme Marceau will look after you well, I am sure.'

'Many thanks for your help. Good-bye for now.'

He let in the clutch and drove slowly out from the forecourt of the garage into the High Street. He negotiated the narrow bridge, with its ancient and moss-covered stones, very carefully, mounted the hill and turned off into what had once been the front garden of a gracious flint and timbered house and was now the car-park of the Crown Hotel.

He parked his car neatly at one side and went in to book a room.

Mme Marceau was a motherly type, with plump and kindly features.

'Yes, m'sieu—of course. We have plenty of room—the season is practically over. I can give you the main room on the front with the four-poster bed in which Henri of Navarre slept before he became the King of France. Not many people stay here. Vallorme is too remote. We specialize rather in good food. Would you be in for lunch?'

'No, thank you, madame—I shall not have time. But dinner tonight—that is another matter. Since you have told me your speciality is good food I am profoundly interested. What time would you like me to be here?'

She smiled at his eagerness.

'Seven o'clock. Punctually, if you please. It is only fair to the cook. Who is me.'

'I agree with you entirely, madame. I shall be in your

dining-room at seven. Thank you very much. Good-bye for now.'

He decided to walk back to the town to see Inspector Frey. There was a lot to be done—he would have to interview all the individuals he had seen coming out of the copse earlier that morning—but in a small place like this he would be almost as quick on foot.

If he got busy he would have to swallow a hasty sandwich. Once his work had been done, conscientiously and well, and in keeping with his own rigid and unyielding standards, then he could relax and thoroughly enjoy a gargantuan meal at the hotel. He sensed with complete conviction that the dinner would be something exceptional— Mme Marceau had made a profound impression on him.

The fact that he had endured the nervous tension of driving fast for hours without stopping for any breakfast he had completely forgotten.

This was no accident. This was murder. This was one more new case he was going to solve. This was one more step up what fate decreed was going to be a very long ladder—but this, mercifully, he did not know. He was filled with a supreme self-confidence. This was important. This was his whole life. There was no time to worry about things like food and regular meals when there was so much work to be done, so many problems to consider, so many plans to be made . . .

In later years he was to pay dearly for this unthinking abuse of his digestive tract—to pay with an agony of mental and physical suffering he would never forget.

But now he was young—not only young but blessed with exceptional strength and tremendous energy, and inspired by the unassailable conviction of his own capabilities.

With the easy acceptance of youth he took for granted the indisputable fact that he had been endowed with a stomach fully capable of digesting whatever he put into it, a throat to swallow any amount of liquor and a virility both to copulate and reproduce. This was nothing more than a fact. No one argued with facts.

4

Inspector Frey was small and dapper, neat and compact. His features were thin and earnest, his forehead high and intellectual.

He stood up from behind his desk and waved M. Pinaud to a chair.

'Please sit down, M'sieu Pinaud,' he said quietly. 'I have had your chief on the telephone this morning.'

The alert and decisive voice was not only quiet but completely without expression. He might have been commenting on the weather.

'Thank you.'

M. Pinaud sat down. The chair was comfortable—far too comfortable. He shifted his position and sat on its edge.

'Provided you have no objection, m'sieu—' he said politely, allowing his voice to die to make a question of the statement.

'Objection? How can I have any objection? We all feel privileged here that co-operation should have been requested. After all, the Paris *Sûreté* are amongst the élite, are they not?'

A charming smile softened the intense earnestness of his features. M. Pinaud smiled in response.

In about twenty years' time, he thought swiftly, the inspector would be able to add: and you, M'sieu Pinaud, are its most celebrated and renowned detective. It will be both a privilege and an honour to work with you. But twenty years of hard work, with all their dangers and risks and narrow escapes from death at present lay between them and that unspoken remark. At the moment he was a junior detective, a nobody. M. le Chef was the élite to whom the inspector referred. He sighed philosophically and answered the question.

'They have that reputation,' he agreed. 'I myself have only recently joined and therefore I can claim no credit.'

They continued to smile at each other for a moment and then the inspector spoke again. This time he did not smile.

'As I said, I cannot possibly have any objection to your chief's request, M'sieu Pinaud. But all the same I fail to understand why he should ask for it. This obscure local accident—'

M. Pinaud, too, decided that the time for smiling amicably at each other was over, and therefore interrupted him and got down to business without compunction.

'Are you sure it was an accident?'

Inspector Frey looked extremely surprised.

'Of course I am sure. It happens all the time. Fools go out shooting with a loaded gun under their arm with the safety-catch off so that they can fire in a matter of seconds. One can stumble, one misplaced step—and there you are. Finished.'

'Maybe. But it is a chance in a million that the gun should fall in the one position.'

'I do not agree with your mathematics,' the inspector told him coolly. 'Unlikely is perhaps a better word. But not impossible. No, indeed. It has happened before and no doubt will happen again.'

'This one should never have happened,' M. Pinaud replied with positive conviction, and was about to tell him about the rope marks he had seen around a tree when the inspector answered him with one word which was uttered with a conviction as positive as his own.

'Nonsense.'

There was silence for a moment. M. Pinaud thought then that there was not much point in sharing the knowledge of his only piece of evidence if this was the mental attitude that would receive it. Far better to keep it to himself at this stage and see what happened next.

'Why do you say that?' he asked quietly.

The inspector had the grace to look somewhat contrite and even apologized.

'I am sorry, M'sieu Pinaud—but while I am eager to help you and will do everything possible in my power to do so, I am afraid I think that this whole idea of collaboration and co-operation is, as I said, complete and utter nonsense.'

'I am sorry too,' M. Pinaud replied, 'but I disagree with you. My reasons at this stage are not important. Let us just say for the moment that I am not satisfied, and leave it at that. So that now we can get on amicably together and you can give me some of this help you so kindly promised.'

He smiled once again and this time it was the inspector who responded.

'Excuse me,' he said and got up out of his chair. He crossed the room to a cupboard against the far wall, opened the door, and brought out a bottle of brandy and two large glasses. He set them all on the desk. Then he uncorked the bottle swiftly and efficiently and filled both glasses to the brim.

'You are quite right,' he said very slowly, sipping a small amount of brandy between each word he enunciated. 'Let us get on with what we have to do.'

The inspector waited for a moment in silence, giving M. Pinaud a chance to taste his brandy, accepted a cigarette from the proferred pack, and then replaced his empty glass on the desk.

'What do you suspect, then?' he asked.

'Murder.'

'Impossible. Unthinkable.'

'Why?'

'Well—granted that he was perhaps the most hated man in town—'

'Ah, yes,' M. Pinaud interrupted quickly. 'Everyone I have met seems to make a point of telling me that. This fact should be of some help. Perhaps to both of us. It is nearly always in the character of the victim that we find a clue to the murderer. But I am sorry—I interrupted you—what were you about to say?'

'It does not matter. I was going to add that even if this were so and someone had decided to kill him, who would be lunatic enough to do it in broad daylight, in a place where several people were almost sure to be walking about shooting rabbits at that time and at this season? The risk of being seen—'

He shrugged and did not finish the sentence, refilled their glasses and drank some more brandy.

M. Pinaud waited to make sure that he was not interrupting again before he spoke.

'That copse is extensive,' he said mildly, 'and apart from the tracks, practically impenetrable. I know. I have been there. I saw the place where he died. And besides, the most unlikely place is always the best one to commit a murder, especially if it is going to be accepted as an accident. Only I do not accept it.'

'Very well. What do you think, then?'

'I think that any one of the four men who spoke to me coming out of that copse might well have killed him. They all carried shotguns of the same bore as his. As I said before, for quite a period of time the firing was almost continuous. It need not have been his own cartridge that killed him.'

The inspector nodded thoughtfully, frowning with concentrated thought.

'I see. It is a theory. It is a good theory. Have you any evidence or proof to support it?'

M. Pinaud decided to tell him. After all, he was the Inspector of Police in Vallorme, and if he was going to provide co-operation and help he would have to know.

'Yes. I found marks on the bark of a young tree which could have been made by knotting a rope or a cord tightly around it. Just in the right place, behind his body. This could have been concealed in the grass and leaves across the track and the other end pulled up sharply to trip him up. There are enough bushes and shrubs on that side to give complete concealment.'

'Have you got the rope?'

M. Pinaud looked at him with exasperation.

'It is hardly likely that the murderer would have left it—'

'I know. I know. But that would have been proof. Proof positive. Your marks on the tree may be evidence—but completely useless evidence.'

'Why?'

'Because a clever lawyer for the defence would ridicule them in a crowded court without the slightest difficulty— quoting all the other things that might easily have caused them—the teeth of rabbits, a sharp heavy branch falling in a high wind, the teeth of squirrels, a man's heavy shooting boots kicking after he had relieved himself against the trunk, the teeth of rats—that copse is alive with game and vermin—I could go on, as he surely would, for a long time. Everyone in the court—including the judge—would listen spellbound, regardless of time, fascinated by his eloquence. You must not let your imagination run away with you, M'sieu Pinaud. Now what about fingerprints on the guns?'

M. Pinaud shook his head.

'If my theory is right, each gun will only have one set of fingerprints—its owners.'

'What about Colonel Romand's gun?'

'If the murderer used that one, either to shoot him in the back of the head, or to discharge the cartridge in the air

70

afterwards, he would surely have used gloves. Which means that the only prints on that gun will be those of its owner, his daughter and his wife.'

Seeing the inspector's puzzled look he continued to explain.

'The daughter was frightened that there might be another accident. The other barrel was still loaded. She picked up the gun and took it to her mother, who unloaded it, cleaned it and put it back on its rack in the gun-room as a matter of course.'

For a long moment there was silence. Both men contemplated their glasses but did not drink.

'I see,' said the inspector at last, very slowly and thoughtfully. 'So what it really amounts to is that you have no evidence and no proof at all to uphold your theory of murder?'

'None at all,' agreed M. Pinaud readily, his voice completely expressionless. 'But I know I am right. And I know that I shall get some. That is why I need your help. I need more information. May I ask you some questions?'

'Of course.'

'Thank you. First of all, the place—this copse, through which Mme Romand told me there is a medieval right of way—surely it is unusual for all these people I met there to be shooting on private land—'

The inspector had reached for his glass as he started

speaking and had already sipped an astonishing amount of brandy before he interrupted.

'Extremely unusual, M'sieu Pinaud. I agree with you. But nevertheless it is one of those things that do happen, particularly in a small and isolated town like this one of Vallorme. A relic of the past, continuing unchanged in modern times. Mme Romand's family and ancestors have lived in that house for centuries and the privilege has remained, exercised and never rescinded, as a part of local law ever since it was granted. If you are interested you could probably find all the details, dates and reasons in some of the archives kept in the Town Hall.

'Over the years, naturally, every local inhabitant who walks through the copse with a gun under his arm—since it abounds in game—will swear with a frank, honest and open conviction that he keeps strictly to the paths to which he is entitled and only fires at whatever crosses them, understanding fully and completely and with grateful recognition that he is walking through private land only by the courtesy of Mme Romand and her ancestors.

'This, at present, is the *status quo*. No one has ever bothered to change it.'

He paused. M. Pinaud reached for his glass. It was superlative brandy.

'I see. Now the people I met this morning coming out of it—no—let us begin with the dead man.'

The inspector replaced his own glass on the desk, declined politely the offer of another cigarette from the outstretched pack and brought out a pipe and pouch from his pocket.

'Very well.'

He made quite a performance of filling and lighting his

pipe and appeared to be thinking profoundly all the time he was doing it, frowning in concentration. Then, puffing out clouds of smoke, he began to speak, choosing his words with obvious care.

'It is rather difficult to express this in words, M'sieu Pinaud. But let me try to put you in the picture. As I said before, this is a small town and we all know each other—and each other's business, somewhat naturally. And we have all lived peacefully and happily together here for a long time. There is no crime here in Vallorme, apart from the usual petty offences occurring in any community of people. My job here is a joke.

'A few months ago Colonel Romand resigned from the Army, which we all understood was to have been his career. He gave out that he resigned—but none of us believed him. It is far more likely that there was some kind of scandal—but there is no proof. The Army Council does not approve of misbehaviour by its high-ranking officers and the War Office never discusses such matters—so there can be no proof. But since he retired and came to live here the whole atmosphere of this town changed for the worse. There were undercurrents and tensions of emotion and behaviour which seem to have polluted and poisoned much of the clean and happy life we once enjoyed together. Before he came.'

'What do you mean?' asked M. Pinaud quietly.

There was no hesitation in the reply.

'I mean that he was an evil and depraved character—a throwback such as is sometimes spawned by these ancient and inbred families—and in addition, I am positive, a sexual maniac, a pervert and a paedophile.'

There was a long and—to M. Pinaud with his vivid

imagination—somehow horrifying silence. The inspector smoked placidly on for a while and then continued.

'There is no actual proof—but we talk and we gossip and we discuss, as people who know each other do in any small town—but unless some specific complaint is made to me, I can do nothing within the law. And no one has said anything openly.'

He paused again and refilled their glasses. M. Pinaud did not say anything. He was listening attentively.

'The one we pitied above all was his wife. She is a good and tragic person, I believe some relation—a first cousin—to our local Dr Justeron. It is a known fact that she only married the colonel to be able to continue to provide a home for her daughter Claudine. She would do anything for that girl, whom she idolizes. But that was the one thing she should not have done. She should have known better.

'On the other hand, mind you, he could be incredibly charming, courteous and fascinating company when he chose. He was a cultured, well-read and widely travelled man. And she was always a rather unworldly type, brought up very strictly in a convent and a sheltered home. Claudine's father, her first husband, was killed in a farming accident when the child was younger, and there was never very much money. Certainly not enough to pay for the upkeep and the maintenance of that house.

'I am sure she married him deliberately—with only that in mind. He was the model of a country gentleman when he first arrived here, let it be known that he was looking for a house and began to entertain at the Crown Hotel, which, as you probably know, is famous for its *cuisine*.

'Now that he is dead, she will be the first one to know

happiness again—the first and most important one of several. For her this must be a truly happy day.'

'Yes,' M. Pinaud told him. 'Those were her very words to me. After looking at his face I felt I could understand. Also—not knowing any of them—I wondered how he could have fathered a girl like Claudine. Now you have explained.'

Then there was another silence.

The inspector laid down his pipe and reached for the bottle to refill their glasses. He tilted it in his hand with a look of resignation, stood up in one swift movement and went to the cupboard, from which he returned with a new one in his hand, all without saying a word.

M. Pinaud contemplated his actions with a benign approval. Nothing like this could have possibly happened in any office in the *Sûreté*. It seemed that only in these remote and isolated districts was the true art of combining business with pleasure so efficiently appreciated and practised.

He ignored the ominous mutterings and rumblings from his sadly neglected intestines as they tried, sternly but vainly, to remind him that the last food he had given them to digest had been on the previous evening—after all, there were so many other more important things to think about when endeavouring to solve a murder case.

He sat up even more rigidly on the edge of the chair.

'Thank you very much. This is really a magnificent

brandy. Now then—about the people who were shooting in that place at the same time—those who came out and spoke to me while I was changing my wheel. There were four. The first one was short and thickset and I should think immensely strong. He had close-cropped hair and a terrific roaring voice. Ulysse Dumont the name he—'

'I was just about to give it to you,' the inspector interrupted, smiling. 'After your description there can be no doubt. Besides, it is a well-known fact that at this season of the year he is poaching in that copse nearly every morning. He is not the type to respect or pay any attention to medieval rights of way, nor to keep to a path if he sees a rabbit somewhere else. This is a known and accepted fact. No one says anything about it.'

'Why not?'

The smile vanished suddenly from the inspector's mouth.

'Perhaps because we are all on his side. Colonel Romand treated him abominably. Dumont is a simple man at heart. Maybe he feels that he is getting some of his own back.'

He settled more comfortably in his chair and placed his fingertips together.

'These are the facts. Dumont is a woodsman and gardener. He and his ancestors before him have lived for generations in a small cottage on the other side of the estate, at the edge of the forest, which belongs to the property. He has always looked after the trees and kept the garden from neglect if ever the house was closed. Mme Romand was the only daughter and the last of her line.

'Some months after she re-married and Colonel Romand went there to live he sent for Dumont and told him that he had no further need of his services. He preferred to attend to the garden himself and he had decided to sell the forest as it stood to a development company. He could do nothing about the cottage, because fortunately Dumont owned that. Dumont has never told anyone what he said in reply.

'Then his young daughter, still at school, became pregnant. She refused to name the father. We all had a very shrewd idea as to who he was, but without her co-operation there could be no proof. No one could persuade her—not even Dumont—to give his name.

'Dumont took her to Dr Justeron, who apparently gave them both good advice, put Dumont's money back into his hand, and declined to earn it the way that Dumont had suggested. He is a good type, that doctor. We all like him.

'So Dumont spends some of his hard-earned money on two railway tickets to Paris, where these matters happen perhaps rather more frequently and therefore present no difficulty.

'But he came back the next day with most of it still in his pocket, because when he got out of the train to buy a newspaper on the platform at Lyons, she slipped out of the compartment, took a local train to a small town called Callaume and there threw herself, quickly and efficiently, in front of the down express, which was travelling at about one hundred and fifty kilometres an hour on the straight stretch—long before it began to slow up for Lyons.

'Here in this town there is no blame for him—only pity. His wife died many years ago. And however much sympathy and understanding there may be between a child and a father who worships her, this inevitably diminishes and even dies with the onset and the psychological problems of puberty.

'Dumont was so upset at her condition that he almost certainly handled the whole situation in the worst possible way. He even told someone after a few drinks that he had used his belt to thrash her, to try to get the name of the man responsible.'

He paused and sighed profoundly. Then he looked up at M. Pinaud frankly and directly.

'That is why we all pity him,' he added quietly. And in his voice there was a dignity and a sympathy which compelled respect.

For a moment M. Pinaud did not answer. He was profoundly impressed by what he had heard. But pity and tolerance, he thought swiftly, might well be two estimable and commendable virtues, and yet in his mind at that time they formed even less than a background.

He was young and eager, conscientious and loyal to his duty as he saw it. He was a detective officially engaged in investigating a case of murder.

A woodsman's cord would have been eminently suitable for tying around a young tree.

He carefully kept all expression from his voice when he replied.

'Yes,' he said quietly. 'You are right. He has had a raw deal. I will have a talk with him later—and with all the others. Now the next one. A young chap with a reddish beard and moustache, inclined to a paunch. Name of David Marbon, I was informed. Told me he was a traveller and had the same make of car as mine.'

'Yes,' the inspector replied. 'He is away on business

from Monday to Friday nearly every week, which is not a good employment for a man with a young and attractive wife and two small children. He works hard, to give him his due, for their sakes, but from all accounts he is not very successful. There is not much money coming into that household.

'He would find a few rabbits in his larder a welcome change from the butcher's bill. Most of his commission goes to pay the mortgage on the new house he bought when they married. It is one of a small development which has been put up on the site of the old water-mill, down by the river. Number 14, I think.'

He paused for a moment, looked at his empty glass longingly, and then placed his fingertips together again very firmly and contemplated them with an air of righteous self-satisfaction.

'I would like you to realize, M'sieu Pinaud,' he continued rather more slowly, 'that what I am about to tell you is only local gossip and rumour. There is no proof. But apparently the light in the main bedroom of that new house has been seen switched on for hours, very late at night, several times while David Marbon has been away travelling.'

He paused again and looked up attentively, but M. Pinaud made no comment.

'Now I have no hesitation in telling you that I listen both to local gossip and to local rumour. That is part of my job. That is how I can prevent a certain amount of crime before it happens.

'And my comment on this kind of talk is that if a young wife was doing her own job conscientiously by looking after two small children, not having very much money to spend and therefore unable to afford a maid, with all the work of cooking their meals and washing-up, the washing, ironing and mending of their clothes, playing with them and keeping them happy, amused and interested—to say nothing of all the cleaning and housework—then—logically each evening she should fall into bed completely exhausted and sleep like the dead. If she had the light on to read it would not be for long. Most young wives with children do not even have time to look at the morning newspaper until they are tucked up into bed.'

He stopped speaking, looked at the idleness of his fingertips and hands with a pained expression of wondering approval and used them immediately to refill their glasses.

M. Pinaud thanked him politely and offered his cigarettes again.

'Thank you,' he said quietly, as memories of his own marriage, vivid and poignant and frustrating, surged swiftly to flood his mind with the instantaneous wonder of thought. 'I agree with everything you say. And you have confirmed not only what he told me himself but also my own impression of him even before he told me—that here was a very worried young man—one with a problem on his mind.'

'Indeed he had. Then. But no longer. Which goes to prove that my theory of an accident is correct.'

'What do you mean?'

'I mean that if it were an accident, then he could not possibly have known about it. Therefore when he came out of the copse and you saw him, he would still have had his problem on his mind. That is why he looked worried. If he had shot Colonel Romand, who was quite likely his wife's lover, as you suggest he might have done, he would surely have looked pleased. His problem was solved.'

'Not at all,' replied M. Pinaud coolly. 'Killing a man,

almost certainly for the first time, is no light matter, especially for a young man. He would have been more worried than ever, wondering now whether he would ever be found out.'

He paused long enough to drink some more of that exquisite brandy.

'Besides,' he continued quietly, 'you yourself, by what you have just told me, are the one who is confirming my theory of murder, as opposed to yours of an accident. I spoke to four men this morning, all of whom were in the copse at the time. The first two I have mentioned I now learn are obviously both prime suspects. Murder has often been committed with far less justification than these two had.

'And for your information—in spite of the butcher's bill— this David Marbon did not shoot any rabbits. He told me—by way of explanation—that he had too much on his mind to concentrate.

'Now let us get on with the next one. No name, but a beautiful black retriever dog called Nero.'

'There is only one in the town. He belongs to Louis Brevin. Tall and lean and handsome, long black hair and light grey eyes—'

'That is the one.'

The inspector considered for a moment very thoughtfully. When he spoke, his voice was quiet and without expression. What he said was surprising.

'Then that brings the number of your suspects up to three, M'sieu Pinaud.'

'Why?'

'Because there are only two loves in the whole of Louis

Brevin's life. One is Claudine Romand and the other is his dog Nero.

'He has been in love with Claudine ever since they were at school together. He bought Nero two days after the dog was born, which made it three days after Mme Romand told him that there could be no question of marriage until Claudine was several years older.

'There was then no idea or mention of any objection to him as a suitor. No one can have any objection to Louis Brevin. He is a highly commendable young man, already assistant manager at our local bank and due for transfer and promotion to their head office at any moment, simply because of his exceptional ability. He was left an orphan at an early age, and somewhat naturally wishes to have his own home and family as soon as possible.

'He is a young man of splendid character and outstanding prospects. He is intelligent enough to understand and appreciate Mme Romand's point of view and to realize that her motivation was only due to her own overwhelming love for her child. That was something he could appreciate. And then, probably inspired by another facet of the same motive, she married Colonel Romand, and immediately things became difficult.'

The inspector took another sip of brandy and his voice suddenly changed.

'Are you in a hurry, M'sieu Pinaud? Am I boring you?'

M. Pinaud looked at his own glass and saw with astonishment that it was empty. The inspector intercepted his glance and immediately rectified the matter.

'Thank you. The answer is no—definitely no—to both your questions. I am not in any hurry. I am doing my work here, for which I am being paid. How could I be in a hurry—while you are giving me this incredible brandy? And I certainly am not bored. On the contrary, I find your information regarding these characters both fascinating and absorbing. Please continue.'

'Good. Well—these two met, naturally, and apparently it was a case of cat and dog at first sight. They hated each other from the beginning. Colonel Romand may have had other plans for his stepdaughter, in spite of his wife's wishes, which it soon became common knowledge he completely ignored.'

His voice softened as he spoke the next sentence, and the complete absence of expression with which the words were uttered seemed to M. Pinaud to make their implication even more horrifying.

'Or there may have been a deeper, more furtive and even more shameful reason—you must judge for yourself.

'Whatever his motivation, the colonel did everything in his power to hinder, thwart and obstruct Louis Brevin in the courtship of his stepdaughter.

'He intercepted and destroyed their letters and denied it strongly when he was accused. He deliberately misinterpreted telephone messages so that they wasted whole evenings waiting for each other in the wrong places and apologized profusely afterwards for his mistakes. He told lies about the one to the other—he did everything he possibly could to make them unhappy.

'In the end he listened to what Louis Brevin had to say, refused to give his consent to either an engagement or a marriage—which he had the right to do, since Claudine is still under age—and then forbade him to come to the house again.'

The inspector paused to knock out his pipe into a large ashtray. Then he began to fill it again.

'So here is one more,' he continued, 'for whom this tragic accident will make a happy day.'

'Yes,' M. Pinaud agreed. 'And as you so rightly said, here is one more suspect for me.'

'I said it,' the inspector replied quickly, 'because I can see how your mind is working. But I do not necessarily believe it myself. It is a well-known fact that Louis Brevin has been in that copse nearly every morning since the season began, hoping perhaps that one day Claudine would find enough energy to get up sufficiently early so that he could see her.'

'That may be. But it does nothing to alter the situation. I will see him after the others. Now there is only one more. Dr Justeron.'

The inspector lit his pipe, puffed out clouds of smoke and looked at him with an astonishment bordering on stupefaction.

'But surely—you can't possibly mean—'

'Why not?' M. Pinaud interrupted calmly. 'He also came out of the copse. He had a gun under his arm as well. You told me he was some relation of Mme—'

'But he is our local doctor—he always has been, ever since I came here. He acts as our police surgeon whenever necessary. He will examine the body and fill in the official report for the—'

'That is normal procedure in a small town. But just as in the case of Louis Brevin—it does not alter the situation. It is often—'

'But this is unthinkable. This is monstrous.'

The inspector jumped to his feet without ceasing to talk.

'Dr Justeron is a healer—a dedicated and selfless man—everyone in this town has the highest regard for his—'

'That may be. You know him. I am a stranger here. I do not dispute what you say. I am only concerned with the facts. Inspector Frey—I think it is time we stopped interrupting each other and I got on with my work.'

M. Pinaud stood up and held out his hand.

'May I thank you for your willing co-operation, which I am sure I shall find invaluable, and also for your hospitality and the most excellent brandy I have tasted for years. I can only hope that I have not taken up too much of your time.'

The inspector shook his hand reluctantly, as if in a daze. Considering the amount of brandy he had consumed, this was hardly surprising.

'Of course not. I am glad if I have been able to help. Would you care for another drink?'

'No, thank you. I will be seeing you again, no doubt. Good-bye for now.'

5

Pinaud, he told himself severely, the whole morning seems to have flown by and nothing has been achieved apart from a good deal of talk. You do not seem to be making much progress. It is time you did something.

And now you are ravenously hungry, which is not surprising. But there is no time to eat. You have work to do.

He called in at the nearest café and purchased two huge ham sandwiches, which he sprinkled and spread liberally with red pepper and mustard. Munching and swallowing mouthfuls of these with a wolfish rapidity as he walked, he set off down the High Street towards the house of the late Colonel Romand, continuing to castigate himself, as was his habit, in complete silence and with even more than his usual severity.

You will now be able to reassure Mme Romand that she was right and that Inspector Frey is not greatly concerned with any fingerprints that should have been on her husband's gun. And it might perhaps be wise to have a few words with that lovely daughter of hers, if she has recovered from her shock and fright, and before she has a chance to see Louis Brevin and tell me some plausible tale which he will instruct her to repeat to me.

And by eating in this way as you walk you are not only saving time but also absorbing—you hope—some of that considerable amount of brandy with which you have just filled your empty stomach.

You must never forget to be honest with yourself, Pinaud, he said silently and severely, spitting out a portion of the pig which should never have been included in a sandwich, whatever else you fail to do. To thine own self be true. That was another thing his head-master had once told him. Association of ideas reminded him again of the obligation to use his strength more in controlling his desires than in fulfilling them, and quite unconsciously the severity of his silent voice increased.

You know very well, Pinaud, That Mme Romand does not need the slightest reassurance with regard to any fingerprints on the gun. She told you quite calmly and openly that she had wiped them off herself and that she was quite sure that Inspector Frey would not worry.

And you also know something else—which even a congenital idiot could deduce—and that is that even if her lovely daughter has fully recovered from her shock and fright, no one will ever tell you until she has had a chance to talk to her suitor, Louis Brevin . . .

In this frame of mind he came to the house, wiped his

fingers and hands carefully on a clean handkerchief, and lifted the knocker.

And as the door opened and Claudine smiled at him, he knew exactly why he had come . . .

She wore a very thin and almost transparent robe loosely belted with a sash round her magnificent body and obviously nothing beneath. What little he could not see his imagination found no difficulty in visualizing.

As before, he was amazed at the magnetism of her sex-appeal, and as he looked at her he felt a sudden and almost uncontrollable spasm of lust swelling at his groin with a desire intense enough to border on pain.

She looked him up and down, slowly and meaningfully, and the invitation in her eyes was open and frank and unashamed.

He made a great effort to control himself.

'How are you feeling now, Claudine?' he asked her cheerfully. 'Do you mind if I call you Claudine?'

'Much better, thank you, M'sieu Pinaud. I had a good sleep. Why not? All my friends do. Please come inside.'

She held the tall white door open wide.

'Thank you. I really came to see your mother. Is she in?'

Liar, Pinaud, he told himself as soon as he had uttered the words. You are a first-class liar. If there were a prize awarded for telling the best lie to young girls you would undoubtedly win it.

Instead of answering, she turned and led the way into the living-room, where she sat down gracefully in an armchair and crossed her legs. The robe slipped apart. She made no attempt to close it.

'Then you are unlucky,' she said quietly. 'Or perhaps unexpectedly fortunate—it depends on your point of view. She has gone to see Father Lafarge. She always talks to him for hours. I am not expecting her back for a long time.'

The meaning and the implication in her words were obvious and unmistakable, but in some strange and exciting way they did not detract from the intensity of her provocative appeal but only seemed to add to its unique charm.

With some considerable difficulty he managed to sit down on the very edge of a hard chair opposite.

She looked at him and laughed. Miraculously, her laughter still held all the joy, the abandon and the happiness of childhood. And incredibly, even some of its innocence. Suddenly that thought, even as it came to him, seemed somehow terrible, and a spasm that might have been of pain softened the hard strong lines of his mouth.

'Don't be silly,' she said, patting invitingly the soft and luxurious velvet of the arm of her chair. 'This one is much more comfortable. If you sit on the arm you will be just the right height. I'll show you some of the tricks he taught me. And then we can finish upstairs in my bed.'

The small soft tip of her tongue protruded and circled her wide and passionate mouth wetly and provocatively.

For a long and somehow tragic moment there was silence between them, while all his thoughts, chaotic and confused, angry and sad, seemed to fly together down a long and unending tunnel of horror . . .

He knew to whom she referred. Inspector Frey had already hinted at it a short while ago that now seemed to be hours.

He thought of his wife and he remembered his own children.

And being young and ambitious and filled with a natural concern about his career, he wondered what M. le Chef would have to say if Mme Romand did not talk to Father Lafarge for as long as usual and the news eventually came to him—as it undoubtedly would—that one of his most promising, dedicated and competent detectives had been found copulating with a young girl who was almost certainly under the age of consent whilst engaged—during the firm's time and on an expense account—in the investigation of a murder case . . .

That was another thought—confused and intermingled with all the others—almost too awful to contemplate.

'Look,' he said suddenly, trying desperately to regain control of the situation and fighting with all his strength to subdue the greatest temptation he had ever encountered in his life. 'Look—let us forget what you just said. I would like to talk to you about Louis Brevin.'

She continued to look at him, calmly, coolly, appraisingly and invitingly. Her voice did not change as she replied.

'If that is the only thing you want to do just now—then you will forgive me if I say that I think you are and must be completely mad.'

She shifted around restlessly in the chair, uncrossed her legs and re-crossed them again. The loose sash gaped open even more widely and her nakedness was fully revealed.

'There is nothing to talk about,' she continued, 'with regard to Louis Brevin. He and I were childhood sweethearts, as everyone in this town knows. Now he wants to marry me, and comes sniffing around here in exactly the same way that his dog Nero sniffs around him. He is a good type. There is nothing wrong with him. I am quite willing to marry—if only to get out of this place and settle down to a little peace. And, besides,'—here she smiled at him, with a degree of instinctive and primitive wickedness he had never encountered before—'I have been told that the correct thing to do is to marry a man who has to work for his living. One is then left in comparative isolation—free to do all the things one wants to do, without so much questioning or interference.'

He looked at her with sadness and pity, and a wonder that was poignant in its intensity. In spite of her body, she was still a child. Never before in his comparatively short life had he met such a character. The tragic part of it all was that he saw only too clearly how different it could have been—how different it ought to have been. If only she had never had a stepfather . . .

'Louis wants to marry me,' she continued, 'but he would not hear of it. They did not like each other.'

For the second time, he noticed, she referred to her late stepfather as he, and not by any other name. He opened his mouth to ask her why, but she forestalled his question by continuing to speak.

'He tripped over a root this morning and his gun went off and blew out the back of his head. The world is now a cleaner and better place. I am perhaps the only person who knows how true that is. I am prepared to swear a statement as to what happened to that effect and sign it in any notary's office if anyone thinks it necessary. This morning I was frightened—I have never seen death before—but now I know that a nightmare is over.'

She stood up in one swift and graceful movement, slipped off her robe and sat down again. This time she did not cross her legs but left them spread slightly apart.

'But why are you bothering me with all this talk about Louis? I could not care less. It is you I am interested in. I like you. I like the way you smile with your eyes and not with your mouth. I would like to do things with you. I would like to end up in bed with you. What on earth are you waiting for?'

For the second time he opened his mouth to speak to her and again he closed it. Since this was not a question that could be adequately answered in one sentence, there seemed little point in attempting it.

His thoughts raced on and on. He was literally quivering with desire and passion, but this was a decision so complicated that he could not even begin to understand it himself.

On the one side, he had all his virility, his pride and his manhood—all urging him on to what would have been a logical consummation. On the other, compelling his attention, reflection and consideration, there were so many complex inhibitions, so many memories of his wife, almost sacred in their sweet intensity, so much horror and revulsion at what he had been told . . .

All his problems were suddenly and decisively solved by the sound of a key turning in the lock of the front door.

Claudine snatched up her robe and was out of the armchair with the grace and the speed of a fawn in flight. She was more than halfway up the stairs before the front door began to open.

Mme Romand came slowly into the room and looked at him vaguely for a moment, as if lost and preoccupied in thought.

Then sudden recognition brought animation to her features and vivacity to the brooding and inward seeking eyes.

'Why, M'sieu Pinaud—how did you—of course—Claudine—'

'Here I am, Mother,' the high clear voice interrupted as Claudine came sedately down the stairs.

M. Pinaud was on his feet in an instant, staring in astonishment. A quick combing had brought tidiness to her hair. She wore now a different robe, thick and quilted, tightly belted and full-length, the hem decorously lifted just enough to clear her daintily slippered feet on the stairs.

'Just dashed up for another handkerchief,' she continued coolly and calmly. 'I let M. Pinaud in. As a matter of fact, he came here to see you. I was just trying to entertain him until you came back.'

Perhaps you were dreaming, Pinaud, he told himself silently. You have a very vivid imagination. You could be suffering from hallucinations. It is not possible that this is the same girl.

Aloud he addressed Mme Romand, feeling that perhaps it would be better to look at the pain and sorrow and the suffering in those shadowed eyes which yet tried so bravely to smile, whatever the effort, in order to consecrate the age-hallowed sanctity of the principle of courtesy to a guest— rather than look at her daughter and the laughter and the mockery and even the contempt which he might well see in the crystal-clear depths of those lovely dark eyes.

'I just called in to tell you, madame,' he said quietly, 'that you were quite right about the fingerprints. Inspector Frey, in view of the circumstances of this tragic accident, does not feel that they could have had any significance.'

His voice was quiet, and yet warm with sincerity, sympathy and kindness. He liked this woman, who was so quiet and so sad; he had come to admire her bravery, her courage and her courtesy, now more than ever, after what he had heard about her husband this morning.

And therefore—in spite of his ambitions and his convictions—he made every effort, for this was his nature, to avoid causing her pain.

'That is very kind of you—'

'Not at all,' he interrupted quickly and for a deliberate reason. With such a daughter, and the complications inherent in her character, this one had enough problems of her own without needing to feel grateful or under any obligation to a complete stranger. 'I shall be staying at the Crown Hotel tonight,' he continued before she could speak. 'I have one or two things to do before I go on. If you should need any advice or if you have any problems because of what has just happened, please get in touch with me. I would be glad if I could be of any help.'

For a long moment there was silence. Then her lips quivered and softened, but if it was with a smile there was nothing in it of mirth—only an infinite sadness.

'Thank you, M'sieu Pinaud. You are a kind man. I appreciate your offer, but it will not be necessary. Our problems are behind us now, and no longer in front.'

He noticed that she did not look at her daughter as she spoke, but only at him.

'I am glad—for your sake,' he said simply.

Then he said good-bye very politely and left them together.

According to the neat brass plate on the wall, the surgery was closed, but Dr Justeron opened the front door of the gracious house in the High Street himself, and smiled and held out his hand in welcome.

'Good afternoon, M'sieu Pinaud—welcome to Vallorme. I have heard all about you from Inspector Frey, who came to see me when I was at the morgue just now. Please come inside.'

'Thank you.'

He closed the door and led the way through the hall,

which had been converted with benches, chairs and a glass-partitioned dispensary at one end into a waiting-room, into a small office adjoining and waved a hand towards a chair opposite the desk.

Then he sat down himself.

'As acting police surgeon,' he continued, 'my relations with him are naturally very close. Which is a situation one would expect and entirely as it should be. I have just finished my official report for him after having examined the body.'

He leant forward and picked up a form from the desk.

'Death instantaneous, from the discharge of a heavy bore shotgun at close range. Quite close. An astonishing number of pellets were in the back of his head. Time— about when I saw you outside the copse this morning. From the position of the body when found and the fact that his own gun, with one barrel fired, was lying behind him, the evidence is consistent with the theory that he slipped or stumbled over something on the path and the trigger struck a root or a branch when the gun fell.

'I have therefore put cause of death as accidental and signed it. Carrying a loaded gun under one's arm with the safety-catch off can be dangerous, although I am afraid we all do it. Otherwise one tends to miss the rabbits.'

There was a long silence. This one, thought M. Pinaud, was a cool and competent character. He therefore waited, quite composed, sharing the silence without concern and thinking very carefully what words he would use when he spoke.

'Tell me, Dr Justeron,' he said quietly at length, 'do you think it likely that a man would trip or slip or stumble on a path he would know like the back of his hand, since it ran through his own land?'

The full lips of the wide strong mouth curved in what might have been a smile.

'Not normally—no. But if you were a man like the late Colonel Romand, who was in the habit of drinking brandy for breakfast, possibly—even probably—to drown his conscience, then the answer to your question could well be yes and not no.'

He paused for a moment and then continued.

'Then such a thing becomes possible. More than feasible— and quite likely. So likely that it became a fact. There is no doubt in my mind at all that this is what must have happened. That is why I have signed this death-certificate.'

Again there was a silence. M. Pinaud stirred in his chair.

'I would say that it was a chance in a million that his gun would fall in the direct line with the back of his head.'

The other man's voice was completely impersonal as he answered.

'These things do happen. This one did.'

M. Pinaud looked at him thoughtfully.

'You are not very interested, are you, Dr Justeron?'

'No.'

There was no hesitation in the reply. Again his voice was calm and impersonal, giving away nothing, admitting nothing, sharing his thoughts with no one.

'And you have no regrets?'

'This is not a time for regrets, M'sieu Pinaud, but for rejoicing.'

97

Again his voice did not change, but this time the words themselves seemed to carry their own emotion.

'Inspector Frey has probably told you that I have evidence—'

'Yes,' interrupted Dr Justeron suddenly. In one swift and powerful movement he stood up from his chair, and now as he continued to speak his voice was tense and vibrant with feeling.

'You may call it evidence. But you have no proof. And he also told me that the four of us who were shooting in the copse this morning are all suspect. And that you, with your red-hot Parisian methods, are determined to prove that it was murder by—'

M. Pinaud did not move as he interrupted in his turn.

'Yes.'

Now it was his voice that had become impersonal, completely without inflection, a statement only of fact.

The doctor stared at him as if in complete disbelief. Then he lifted his hands in a gesture that was somehow poignant in its wistfulness. M. Pinaud noticed once more their astonishing beauty and strength before he sat down again, slowly and wearily.

'M'sieu Pinaud,' he said quietly and carefully, 'I ask you in all sincerity—indeed, I beg of you—to let this matter drop. Go back to Paris and leave us in peace. Our small world here is now a cleaner and a better place. Several of us have had more than our share of trouble and unhappiness and have endured our suffering with patience and fortitude. Do not reopen old wounds—which is what you will do if you persist. They are likely to fester. Let them heal.'

There seemed to be only one answer that M. Pinaud could give him.

'We do not like murder at the *Sûreté*, Dr Justeron.'

The doctor looked at him for a long time and there was both pain and suffering in his eyes.

'Nor does anyone,' he said at length. 'I swore the Hippocratic oath, when I was young, to save life, not to take it—but I believe that there is a higher law. And you are the only one who holds the opinion that it is murder, M'sieu Pinaud. Here we all prefer to think of it as an accident—a mercy granted by a divine providence.'

M. Pinaud said nothing, but shook his head.

'Very well.'

'I have my duty.'

'Of course. You must do as you think fit. Let me just tell you a few things that may interest you.'

He paused for a moment, as if to collect his thoughts, and in that brief time, with sudden insight, M. Pinaud sensed some of the horror he was about to hear and shivered as if with cold.

'If you had been called upon to remove the dead body of an unborn child from the womb of a fifteen-year-old girl— if you had seen another, not very much older, aroused to sexual awareness in such a way as to become a nymphomaniac—if you had watched two young children growing up into what may well become psychopaths because their young mother is too occupied with fornication to give them all that love and care and attention which is their right—then you might come to agree with me.'

There was another silence. Then Dr Justeron stood up again and looked down at him thoughtfully.

'I can see that I shall never convince you, M'sieu

Pinaud. You are young and determined and ambitious. But I would be grateful if you could find the time to walk up to the church—it's not far—and see Father Lafarge. He may succeed where I have failed.'

He held out his hand.

'I will see you out. I shall be here if you wish to question me.'

M. Pinaud stood up as well and took the outstretched hand. The doctor's clasp was firm and cool and strong.

He muttered something, followed the doctor to the front door and left the house.

There were so many things he wanted to say, but he could not find the words. The questions could wait. He felt strangely moved by what the doctor had said. He decided to see the priest.

6

Father Lafarge was working in his front garden. The sleeves of his shirt were rolled up to reveal sinewy and rope-like forearms. His cassock was neatly folded on a low stone wall.

He was pruning his roses with loving care, secateurs in one hand, a large flat basket in the other.

He looked up at the sound of footsteps on the road and placed them both down on the grass. A sudden charming smile transfigured the austerity of his lined and ravaged features.

'M'sieu Pinaud,' he said. 'How good of you to come.'

'You asked me to, Father,' replied M. Pinaud quietly.

'I know. I remember. But quite frankly I did not expect you.'

'Why not?'

'Because—unfortunately—in the world as it is today, we live in two different parts of it. They do not meet often enough.'

While he was speaking, the priest had been wiping his hands very carefully on a clean towel which had been folded beside his cassock. Now he came forward and shook M. Pinaud's hand with a warm and vital clasp.

'But you are here. That is enough.'

M. Pinaud looked at him with interest for the second time.

In his shirt-sleeves, bareheaded in the afternoon sun, with the blood dried and congealed from rose-thorns on his hands and wrists, he still seemed to radiate that same astonishing power and grace and authority as when he had worn the clothes that were the symbols of his office. With the sunlight glinting on silver threads amongst that long mane of grey hair, he still held his head like a king without a crown. In his robes in front of the High Altar, M. Pinaud thought, he must have presented a magnificently majestic figure.

'What can I do for you, M'sieu Pinaud?'

His voice was quiet and yet somehow intense with compassion and understanding.

With a start M. Pinaud tried to put order into his thoughts. He realized that they were still standing facing each other and that he had not spoken since he had felt the comfort and reassurance of the priest's right hand.

'I think it would be a good thing, Father, if we might talk a little together, if I do not presume—'

'There can be no question of presumption,' the interruption came swiftly. 'It is your right to ask, and my duty to listen. Here—or inside the church?'

'I, too, have my duty,' M. Pinaud told him quietly. 'It is a very different one from yours. I feel I must talk to you about it. What happened this morning would perhaps be better discussed in the sunshine of this garden, rather than in church.'

The priest looked at him thoughtfully.

'You may well be wrong,' he said at length very slowly. 'Completely wrong. but let it be as you wish. This tragic accident—'

'That is what you called it this morning.'

M. Pinaud's interruption was swift and hard.

'That is what everyone in Vallorme is saying,' he continued. 'But I do not agree. I have just left Dr Justeron. He said—'

'I know what he said.'

This time it was the priest who interrupted him. The voice was no longer compassionate and sympathetic, but as incisive and hard as his own had been.

'You know? How can you know? I have just left—'

'There is very little of what goes on in Vallorme that I do not know.'

This time the priest's voice was quieter and in it there was a courtesy asking for tolerance and understanding.

'This is my town, M'sieu Pinaud,' he continued without a pause. 'This is my parish and these are my people. Each one I have to comfort and strengthen and help. Not as myself, but with the power and the grace of what I represent. I try to be worthy of them. Dr Justeron is a fine and noble man. Just now he is most upset. He telephoned me as soon as you had left.'

'He said that you might be able to convince me.'

'I shall try.'

'To convince me of what?'

The priest looked at him steadily.

'That what happened this morning was a tragic accident,' he replied quietly.

'It was not. You and he and I know it was not. It was murder.'

M. Pinaud's voice was equally quiet. After he had spoken he wondered what had made him say the words.

He knew that he admired and respected the unusual and exemplary character of this man to an unprecedented degree, but everything in his own complex nature—his youth, his enthusiasm, his ambition, his fanatical devotion to his duty—all seemed to be fighting against him, instead of welcoming this man as a counsellor, an adviser and a friend. Perhaps even as the father he could hardly remember . . .

They both waited in the bright sunshine for what seemed to M. Pinaud like a very long time. But never for one second had the regard of those deep-set and steadfast eyes opposite him left his own.

'I prefer,' said Father Lafarge, and to emphasise the deliberation with which he had chosen and pronounced these two words he repeated them. 'I prefer to see it, M'sieu Pinaud, as the hand of God.'

Again, for what seemed an interminable moment, there was silence between them. It seemed suddenly to M. Pinaud as if these silences were sundering them, separating them, dooming them to remain eternally apart in two separate and different worlds which could never become one, however desperately and sincerely they might both reach out to join them, however much they might both dream and desire to make them one . . .

It seemed then to him that they were permitted to share nothing more than the sunshine in its benediction of golden grace, and even that only as strangers by chance met together, knowing that forever they were doomed each to walk a different and separate path . . .

'You are entitled to your opinion, Father,' he said quietly.

'Yes. But you are wrong, M'sieu Pinaud. It is not an opinion. It is a conviction.'

The reply—immediate in its swiftness—reminded him of a thrust of a sword. It held such an intensity that he could almost see the words flashing in the sunshine.

There was another silence. Then M. Pinaud sighed and spoke very quietly.

'I, too, have some of my own.'

'You have evidence, or proof, for them?'

'At present—evidence. Hardly proof. But,' he added without a pause, 'that I will get.'

The words were spoken with a calm and controlled confidence that was more convincing than he knew.

The deep-set eyes studied him thoughtfully for some time, and when the priest spoke again his voice was different, subdued and persuasive and convincing.

'I told you this morning, M'sieu Pinaud, that this Colonel Romand was an evil man who is far better dead. What you may think of me for voicing such an opinion, even if I believed it, is of no importance, for the simple reason that it is not an opinion, but a fact and the truth. I have already prayed for forgiveness for my temerity in voicing it in this way.

'This morning we have both seen the working of a higher law. You yourself may not have had such an experience before—I should think that you are too young—but in my lifetime I have. Not once but several times. When I first saw God strike with His hand I was converted. On subsequent occasions I was convinced in my beliefs. I have seen and learnt enough to know that it is not for mortal man to interfere and thereby cause untold harm and even suffering.'

To anyone passing on the road, two men standing together talking in the sunshine that flooded the beautiful old-world garden. To M. Pinaud, two men standing apart in two different worlds of their own, both infinitely lonely and pathetic in their efforts to understand each other.

He saw in his mind the figure of his headmaster and—again because this priest reminded him so strongly of the past—he heard once more the beautifully articulated words as he read the Sunday lesson to his senior form: 'Render onto Caesar the things which are Caesar's and unto God the things which belong to God.' Expressed so majestically and so logically, the eloquence of the modulated periods sounded so easy . . .

The quiet voice had ceased. In the silence that followed he shook his head slowly.

'Is this what Dr Justeron meant by convincing me?' he asked quietly.

Now it was the priest's turn to shake his head.

'I can see that I have failed,' he replied simply. Then again his voice changed and he spoke with all the intensity of his usual passionate sincerity.

'I beg of you to leave this thing, M'sieu Pinaud. I ask you with humility to renounce this investigation you are so determined on making. Go home—have the love and the compassion to go home—and leave us in the peace some of these unhappy people so richly deserve. Accept the fact that it was purely by chance that you of all people happened to be outside the copse this morning at that particular time, and be thankful that your kindness, courtesy and willingness to help proved of inestimable comfort to a very unhappy woman and her emotionally distraught daughter. Accept the incredibly complicated manifestations of what many people call chance, but for which I, in my sacred calling, have another and better name—accept them and leave it at that.'

There was one moment of almost agonizing silence.

Then the priest stooped and picked up his basket and secateurs. Twice M. Pinaud began to speak and twice he checked himself, because he knew with a strange conviction that had he spoken then the words would not have been the same as those he wished to say . . .

He remembered his headmaster once again, and the words he had spoken then—to thine own self be true—seemed to reverberate in his head as he finally found his voice.

'I am sorry, Father,' he said simply, 'but I must do my duty.'

Which was, after all, only another way of expressing them.

Then he turned and left the priest alone.

The house was small, intelligently designed and cheaply built, with one bedroom over an integral garage, which was now open and empty. The front garden was unusually large and open to view, since the young trees and shrubs planted around the lawn had not yet had time to mature.

M. Pinaud pushed open the gate and walked up the path. Voices and laughter accompanied him as he went.

The little boy was sitting astride an astonishingly realistic wooden railway-engine, brightly painted and mounted on four wheels. The little girl stood up, balancing precariously on the open flat car attached behind.

A young woman, small and dark and intense, in a blouse and very short skirt, was pulling them along by means of what looked like an old clothes-line over her shoulder.

'Puff—puff—puff—bang—a—bang—a—bang,' yelled the small boy ecstatically.

'Chuff—chuff—chuff,' screamed the small girl, dancing and slipping and keeping her balance with a great and violent difficulty.

'Whoo—whoo—whoo,' whistled the motive power of this unorthodox and yet somehow completely convincing method of transportation, hauling energetically on the clothes-line in an effort that clearly outlined her small and provocative breasts through the thin material of her blouse.

Then she saw him and stopped. The train behind her came to a rest. The children's voices ceased abruptly. The silence made him feel guilty.

He held out his hands in a gesture that was almost one of appeal.

'Please—there is no need to stop—I only called to see David Marbon. Forgive me for disturbing you—it is Mme Marbon—is it not?'

She considered him gravely, and yet with a spark of mischief at the back of her intelligent and vivid eyes.

'Yes. I am David's wife. And there is no need to

apologize, M'sieu Pinaud. This is not only a station, but a junction— you can see we have come to the end of the lawn—and trains always stop at stations, don't they, children?'

'Yes—yes—until the signal-disc turns—'

'Of course. Now at this station the engine has to take on water, so you two go on into the kitchen while I talk to M'sieu Pinaud. Milk and cakes are on the table.'

Obediently they left, staring wide-eyed at this stranger who had had the temerity to interrupt their game.

She dropped the clothes-line and turned to face him.

'I am afraid you will not be able to see David now. He has gone to Father Lafarge. He did not tell me why.'

'It does not matter,' he told her quietly. 'I can come back later, or tomorrow. How did you know my name, Mme Marbon?'

She smiled, suddenly and radiantly, and her intense and elfin features were transfigured.

'Because everyone in Vallorme always knows everyone else's business. We know all about you, M'sieu Pinaud, and why you are here. For the same reason I think it would be more advisable not to invite you into the house—as you can see, in this magnificent property we tend to be somewhat overlooked.'

He smiled in response. This was a very charming person, he thought, and nothing like what he had expected.

'Yes,' he said, with no expression in his voice and none on his features. 'You mean that the late light in the bedroom window is already enough to—'

She laughed outright to interrupt him, a happy and completely carefree laugh.

'That would be the old washerwoman, Frey, from the sound of it. Not even I can blame the neighbours for that one. They are all asleep. He is always on duty. But what does it matter? I don't care. My story is that I read a lot in bed. And my library list is evidence that would stand in any court of law.'

'Provided no one saw him come in,' he said gravely.

'Of course not. He used to walk along the river bank when it was dark.'

Nothing of his amazement showed on his features. This frank admission was something he had never expected. His thoughts raced on as he tried to cope with the situation.

'And now that he is dead?' he asked her quietly.

'Now this is the happiest day I have known for weeks and months.'

There had been no hesitation in her reply. She continued without a pause.

'Just wait here for a moment, M'sieu Pinaud, while I fetch two chairs from the garage. I would like to talk to you and we will be more comfortable sitting down here. Then the neighbours will think that you must be the new insurance man.'

She walked away quickly, the short skirt lifting with her stride and revealing a tempting expanse of knee and thigh.

She returned almost immediately and he hastened to meet her, carried the two small folding-chairs on to the lawn and set them up.

'Thank you.'

They sat side by side in the tranquil benediction of the early evening sun. Again she smiled at him. He offered her a cigarette, but she shook her head and continued to smile.

'But please smoke yourself, if you wish. This place is a hot-bed of gossip, M'sieu Pinaud. It would be as well if you got your facts right, whatever you are going to do here. I said I was happy—and believe me I meant it.'

'You sound happy.'

'Because I am. Happier than I have ever been. Now the nightmare is over. Our troubles are finished. Now we can start again—to build a new life with our happiness and not to destroy it even as it festered within. I have no regrets. I only did it for the money. He paid me well. And he got his money's worth—my own self-respect compels me to add. Then I admit it tended sometimes to become somewhat wild. He was such a beast—such a depraved swine—such a lecher.'

She paused for a moment. as if to collect her thoughts. But her eyes, frank and unashamed, continued to meet his own steadily. Then the words seemed to pour out in a sudden torrent, releasing all her pent-up emotion.

'David is like a child in many ways. He built and painted that engine and truck himself for the children. Only a man with the imagination of a child could have made it so beautifully. But in practical matters he is a simpleton. He has no idea of the value of money or what it costs to bring up children. And he is not a very good traveller. Too much of an introvert. To be a good traveller you have got to be interested in other people. You have got to remember to ask, when you go into a shop, how Louise's new baby is getting on and whether the insurance paid for the window the cup-final gang smashed on their way home. To an introvert this comes hard, since he is

111

usually only concerned with himself. Therefore he does not earn anything like an adequate salary. He has enough worries on his mind with business, and so I made up my own and decided to help him.

'Now there is another reason why I am so happy. He has finally made up his mind to listen to other people's good advice. He is leaving his firm and taking a local job, so that he can live a normal life at home here with his wife and family.

'Until quite recently it has been a routine of coming back here late on a Friday night, exhausted and depressed with driving and selling, recovering on Saturday but still too tired to do anything—either to play with his own children or to satisfy his wife in bed—then resting on Sunday in order to go to bed early alone, so as to be fit and ready to leave the house at some unearthly hour on Monday morning for the honour and the glory of his firm. And all for a salary and commission that hardly pay the mortgage on this new house.'

She ceased abruptly and for a long moment there was silence.

Then M. Pinaud moved in his chair and lit another cigarette.

'I see what you mean,' he said quietly. And at the warmth, sincerity and kindness in his voice that sudden and radiant smile transformed her features again.

'You must be a very understanding person, M'sieu Pinaud,' she told him. 'I had no idea I was going to talk and reveal myself like this. I am glad I did. You have been very patient. I hope you will promise me one thing.'

'Of course. What is that?'

112

'Not a word to David—about all this—when you see him.'

'I would not think of it.'

'Thank you. He has been listening to gossip and rumour and lies about me for months now, and I can see that it has driven him nearly mad with anxiety and worry. All the more since he has chosen to bottle it all up inside him instead of asking me.

'I could have explained it all so easily. But he would not ask me. And I have my pride. When the time comes I will tell him the truth, as I have told it to you, and then we will begin to build our new life together.'

'You are quite sure—that he will want to know the truth?'

'Of course. He will understand why I did it.'

He stood up in one swift and sudden movement, a tall and powerful figure with a cat-like grace, and stayed very still, looking down at her small form with a strangely intense gravity.

'He must love you very greatly,' he said gently.

She stood up as well, dwarfed by his height, and yet proud with a great dignity.

'And I him. That is what gave me the strength and courage to endure that swine and his filth. There is only one way to love, M'sieu Pinaud.'

He held out his hand.

'I know. Thank you for your confidence, Mme Marbon. I will call again to see your husband.'

He shook her hand, said good-bye, and watched her walk away to rejoin her children in the kitchen.

He looked at the gaily painted engine very thoughtfully for a moment and then left the garden.

*　　*　　*

He walked back very slowly away from the site of the old water-mill.

Suddenly he felt tired and dispirited. This was a very strange place, he decided.

There were currents and undercurrents of emotion here that he found hard to understand. And none of them seemed to be pointing in any way that would help him to solve the murder of Colonel Romand. Indeed, there were so many people here in this town with good reason to wish him dead that the trail had become confused to the point where reason and logic no longer seemed to apply.

The unanimous and unequivocal acceptance of the shooting as an accident by the priest, the inspector and the doctor held obviously some profound significance, but— think as much as he could—he was unable to see why.

A little while ago he had seen an old clothes-line, tied to a wooden engine, which could well have been tied just as easily to the young tree whose bark he had examined, in order to trip Colonel Romand so that a shotgun could be fired at the back of his head while he was lying helpless on the path.

But if something like that had happened, then why should these three, a priest and two influential citizens of the town, collaborate together to convince him, a stranger, that the death had been an accident? It did not make sense.

He felt tired, dejected and exhausted. But his conscience

drove him on, remorselessly and relentlessly. He could not afford to rest. There was no time to relax. He had not finished yet. He could say with truth that he had not even begun. He was convinced that this was a case of murder, and his duty to find the murderer was clear and unmistakable.

For that he was paid his salary by M. le Chef, and provided with a car. The salary was obviously inadequate, but having accepted it he had also accepted the moral obligation of earning it—fairly, honestly and conscientiously.

And there was no doubt that the car was a very great help. Even with the strict accounting of his mileage and M. le Chef's meticulous checking of his weekly expense-sheet with slide-rule, calculator and comptometer, there was usually enough petrol left in the tank to take his wife shopping when she had a heavy basket and to see her aged mother at the week-end. There were compensations, even for a job which was difficult, exacting and inevitably dangerous. It was up to him to earn his money with dignity and pride.

Now he still had two more suspects to see—Ulysse Dumont, the woodsman and gardener, and Louis Brevin, the man with the dog.

He glanced at his watch. There was still time to see one of them. He must not be late, if he was going to sleep in a bed once occupied by Henri of Navarre and eat an exquisite meal prepared by Mme Marceau, who specialized in good food.

The day had flown by, as if on wings. He remembered that he had hardly slept the night before—which explained his sudden overpowering lassitude. And he remembered those unworthy portions of the pig which that unscrupulous café proprietor had seen fit to include in his sandwich, which accounted for his sudden ravenous and overwhelming hunger.

He did not seem to be making much progress. But his very nature would never allow him to stop trying . . .

7

The woodshed of Ulysse Dumont, built at one end of an integral part of the long low cottage, had once been a stable. Two massive oak beams, centuries old, supported the double door. The lower half was closed, the upper half open.

M. Pinaud rested his elbows on the lower half and looked inside with interest.

The interior was immaculate, a delight to behold. Sawn and massive tree-trunks were neatly piled from the stone-flagged floor nearly to the rafters. Smaller and thinner branches were stacked, neatly and symmetrically, in front of them, the sawn-off edges parallel, the piles orderly. Several bundles of these, he observed, were tied together, as if for delivery, by lengths of thin but obviously very strong cord. Wooden boxes of kindling were stacked in orderly rows against one wall. The floor was swept clear of shavings and sawdust.

Dumont, the sleeves of his flannel shirt rolled up tightly to reveal hairy and muscular forearms, stood beside a neat pile of thick sawn-off logs, chopping each one into billets on a low and massive tree-trunk.

The immense gleaming axe whirled upwards and crashed down, rose again, turned over in mid-air like a feather with the heavy log embedded in it, and crashed down again on the tree-trunk. The log split as easily as a piece of cheese, the two halves flying to either side.

The great resonant voice boomed out in the ensuing silence.

'Ah—ha—the man with the puncture. Come to pay your debts, I presume? I knew you had an honest face—I said so at the time. And I, Ulysse Dumont, am a man who is seldom wrong.'

M. Pinaud sighed and felt in his pocket. With a character like this argument was a waste of time. He held out a five-franc piece and smiled cheerfully.

'You were quite right,' he said pleasantly. 'A builders' nail it was. And so you win your bet.'

'Thank you very much. I knew you had an honest face.'

He picked up another log with two fingers as if it had been a thistle, set it upright on the tree-trunk, spat on his hands and heaved the axe up into the air.

Down it crashed again, the log half-split, up once more to turn over and then down with a terrifying power and force that sent the two halves flying like projectiles to the sides of the shed.

'Now you see why I keep the lower door closed,' he said. 'Sometimes people can get hurt.'

'Don't you want your money?' asked M. Pinaud mildly.

'As you can see, I am busy. Put it on the ledge there, if

you would be so kind. All this pile has got to be finished by tonight.'

'You can still talk while you work, I should think.'

'Yes. That is true. No tongue has ever been created strong enough to swing an axe, as far as I know.'

'Good. Then we can get on. You heard what happened in the copse this morning, when I met you?'

'Naturally. The whole town heard in a very short time. We all know what goes on here.'

'What is your opinion?'

There was a long silence. Dumont opened his hand and the log between his fingers fell with a dull thud to the floor. He leaned on the haft of his axe and looked at M. Pinaud steadily. His eyes were no longer humorous.

'I have no opinion. If I have any feeling, it is one of joy. When vermin are exterminated, it is a matter for rejoicing.'

M. Pinaud reached in his pocket and took out a packet of cigarettes. One hand lifted from the haft of the axe and the gesture was regal and imperative.

'Not in the woodshed—or anywhere near it, if you please.'

M. Pinaud replaced the cigarettes in his pocket with a feeling of guilt and spoke slowly and carefully, choosing his words with care.

'The general opinion in this town seems to be that Colonel Romand met with a fatal accident. The priest, Father Lafarge, Inspector Frey and Dr Justeron all seem to agree on this point. Your use of the word exterminated is interesting, M'sieu Dumont. I am inclined to agree with you. It is time I introduced myself. My name is Pinaud and I work for the Paris *Sûreté*. I have authority, confirmed by Inspector Frey, to investigate this death, which I consider to be a case of murder, and definitely not an accident.'

Dumont had been regarding him steadily all the time he was speaking, his massive hands in tranquil repose on the haft of his axe. But when he finished there was no hesitation in the reply.

'What you consider is your own business, M'sieu Pinaud. Here in Vallorme we prefer to call it an accident. Proving it to be anything else is going to be another matter.'

'I dare say. But I shall do it.'

Something in the way he spoke and uttered the words—something in their supreme sincerity and conviction—made Dumont consider him thoughtfully for a long time. But when he spoke his voice was neutral and non-committal, almost disinterested, quite apart from being very much quieter than before.

'You will find it an impossible task. Dead men tell no tales. Leave it. What have you got?'

'Four suspects who came out of the copse—the scene of the murder—shortly after he was killed there—all carrying shotguns of the same calibre as the one that was fired into the back of his head. Four men who all had good reason to hate him.'

'Nonsense. You are trying to make bricks without straw. Frey came round today to tell me about you. Apparently I am a suspect too.'

M. Pinaud held his penetrating stare steadily.

'Yes—and with good reason—'

'Nonsense again,' Dumont interrupted, his voice now angry and bellowing out at its usual pitch and volume.

'What about all the others who might have been shooting rabbits at the same time? You heard the shots. Wouldn't you have said that there were more than four guns at work? There are other ways in and out of that copse, M'sieu Pinaud, apart from going through the gate or the garden of the house. Those were the ones you did not see. Four of us came out through the gate to where you were changing your wheel. Admitted. Four of us had been shooting rabbits. Who are you, M'sieu Pinaud, to say otherwise?'

'I know nothing about any others,' M. Pinaud told him quietly. 'I only know that the four of you had all good reason to wish him dead.'

Dumont shifted his grip on the haft of his axe, bent down and placed another log on the tree-trunk.

'That is as may be. If that fool Frey were not a gossiping old brandy-soaked washerwoman, you would not know anything about that. And I say nonsense once more. The man's life was a path of filthy and crawling shame, and not many people in this town were liable to escape some of its slime. You have now four names, M'sieu Pinaud. Go to the doctor— he will give you forty.'

His huge and powerful hands shifted and slid down the haft to the correct grip, right hand below left. Suddenly the booming resonant voice softened and quietened again.

'There are certain things, M'sieu Pinaud—thoughts that regret has hallowed and memories sorrow has made sacred— that one does not discuss, whatever the reason or whatever the justification.'

The axe-blade bit gently, almost caressingly, into the log, then swung up, turned over, and crashed down to split it in two at the first stroke.

'Why did you mention the doctor?' M. Pinaud asked him quietly.

'Because he is a man. And he has more sense in his little finger than that idiot Frey has in his whole sodden head. Besides, people always confide in their doctor, don't they?'

The humorous eyes were suddenly grave and shrewd as they met M. Pinaud's frankly.

'He knows most of what goes on in this town,' he added.

'But—'

'Look, M'sieu Pinaud,' Dumont interrupted as he picked up another log, 'it is getting late, and as I told you, I am busy. Tomorrow morning at seven o'clock I shall be tree-felling in the wood behind this cottage. If you want to ask me any questions, come and see me there.'

M. Pinaud looked at his watch and made up his mind.

Dumont was right. It was getting late and he did not seem to be making much progress. He also felt tired and depressed, for that same reason.

It would be nice to have a drink before dinner. And since he had promised Mme Marceau to be punctual, it was obviously imperative that the sooner this drinking business were organized competently the better.

'Very well,' he said, his voice completely expression-less. 'I will do that. See you at seven o'clock tomorrow morning. Good-bye for now.'

Not even the crashing impact of the axe-head on the tree-trunk could drown the great bellowing roar of 'Right—understood' that followed him through the half-open door.

* * *

The large rectangular flagstones on the floor of what was now the lounge in the Crown Hotel had been waxed and polished with loving care for some five hundred years, resulting in an effect commensurate with the devotion inherent in such efforts.

Mercifully, no vandal had thought fit to obliterate such an achievement with a carpet, and therefore one or two small rugs only were permitted to enhance in delightful contrast the gleaming magnificence of each polished stone.

A partition had been built, using contemporary beams in good taste, to convert half of that immense original living-room into the restaurant.

The vast fireplace at one end with its three-metre cross beam remained in the lounge. In it a cheerful log-fire was blazing.

In front of it sat Louis Brevin. He smiled broadly as M. Pinaud entered the room. Nero roused himself in one swift fluid movement and padded across the flagstones to greet him with a low growl of recognition.

M. Pinaud bent to pat his head.

'Hullo there, Nero—what a memory you have. I regret I do not carry my spare wheel about with me.'

Brevin laughed as he stood up.

'Have no fear, M'sieu Pinaud. He is house-trained. The world outside is another matter—fair game to him and all his kind. Would you join me in a drink?'

'Willingly—and thank you,' M. Pinaud replied, straightening up and turning towards the bar in the corner, behind which M. Marceau, a swarthy type with protuberant brown eyes and a wet and loose-lipped mouth, smiled a cheerful greeting. 'But,' he continued, taking out his money, 'as I have a noble and gigantic thirst, and since I am staying here in this hotel, the privilege of paying must obviously be mine. A very large absinthe, if you please, M'sieu Marceau. And you, M'sieu Brevin?'

'That sounds like an excellent choice,' Brevin replied. 'The same for me, please.'

He pulled up another chair near the fire while the landlord was busy. Nero walked back with dignity, half-turned, and sprawled down ecstatically between them.

M. Pinaud brought the drinks and they sat down in front of the fire.

'Your very good health.'

'And yours.'

M. Pinaud sighed with contentment. The absinthe was delicious. It had been a hard and exhausting day, and a very long time since he had enjoyed the inspector's brandy.

From his stool behind the bar, the landlord cast one experienced glance at the level of his glass, lifted the flap of his counter, and appeared in front of them carrying a small table in one hand and a tray balanced on the other. On the tray stood the bottle of absinthe, a bowl of ice and a plate of sliced lemon.

He set the table down carefully well away from Nero, placed the tray on it and smiled happily.

'There, gentlemen. Help yourselves. Since my good wife will not tolerate any unpunctuality in her restaurant, may I remind you that there is now very little time left for serious drinking before seven o'clock. It would therefore be a shame to waste any of it in walking to and from the bar.'

M. Pinaud emptied his glass without delay.

'There goes a man after my own heart,' he pronounced with feeling.

Brevin laughed and followed his example. Then he watched the swift and dexterous movements of M. Pinaud's hands with admiration.

'I agree. He has an axe to grind, but he does it rather well.'

'Very well indeed. Would you care to join me for dinner, M'sieu Brevin?'

During the course of a long and tranquil meal, he reflected, surely he would be able to find out more about this enigmatic young man who was one of his chief suspects.

But Brevin shook his head regretfully.

'Thank you very much—but no. I must go soon. It is Nero's bedtime.'

At the sound of his name the lovely head lifted and the liquid amber eyes gazed adoringly at his master. Brevin leaned forward and the touch of his hand on the dog's head was infinitely gentle.

'Yes, old boy—not long now.'

M. Pinaud looked into his glass.

'Of course. There is a rather nice saying about the dog and his master—'

Brevin flushed and interrupted him gruffly.

'Thank you for the compliment, M'sieu Pinaud.'

'I find it strange,' M. Pinaud continued without any change in the expression of his voice, 'that we two should know each other already, without ever having been formally introduced this morning.'

There was no hesitation in Brevin's reply. His embarrassment had only been temporary.

'Not really,' he said easily. 'This is a small town and

people talk a lot. By now nearly everyone knows who you are and what you are doing here.'

M. Pinaud sipped his drink thoughtfully.

'It is just that which I find so strange,' he replied slowly. 'Everyone knows so much. And I seem to know so little.'

He paused, but there was no reply. He deliberately allowed the silence to prolong itself before he continued.

'Except that everyone seems so happy.'

Brevin lifted his glass and took a gigantic swallow which consumed the greater part of its contents. Then—as perhaps was to be expected—he belched, happily, loudly, defiantly and unashamedly.

'Of course we are happy,' he said calmly. 'Because that arch-bastard Romand is dead. Now this town is a cleaner place. Now some of us can begin to live again.'

He reached out, snapped up his glass and emptied it in one great gulp.

M. Pinaud did not answer. Instead he busied himself with the bottle and the bowl of ice.

Brevin suddenly stood up. Nero did the same.

'No—no—I have had enough—'

'Nonsense,' replied M. Pinaud calmly. 'There is always time to have one for the road. Especially if one is not driving a car.'

In a moment the glass was filled and handed over.

'Thank you very much.'

Brevin drank a little from his glass but remained standing up. He was obviously ready to go home.

'Look, M'sieu Pinaud,' he said quietly and seriously. 'You asked me why I was happy. I told you. But there is another reason. Dr Justeron has told me that he can arrange for Claudine to have special psychological treatment at a clinic he knows in Paris. That is enough to make any man happy.'

There was a short silence while M. Pinaud's mind raced back to his last meeting with Claudine. The very thought of her gave him a surge of sexual desire. He thought, with some deliberation, as to what he should say. And then suddenly he knew.

'You still love her, then? You must love her very greatly.'

And as he said this his voice was quiet and gentle and compassionate.

Brevin put the glass to his lips and finished its contents in one enormous swallow. Then he looked down at M. Pinaud directly, and the light grey eyes seemed to glow with some intense inner light.

'Of course I still love her, M'sieu Pinaud. I have always loved her, since she was a child. There is only one way to love—wholly, unreservedly and completely. Love is an acceptance. There can be no conditions.'

Mme Marceau opened the sliding-door leading to the restaurant.

'Dinner is ready, gentlemen,' she announced.

Brevin turned to go. He bent down to pat Nero's head. The dog had been waiting, quietly and obediently, ever since he stood up.

'Come on, Nero. Time for bed. Thank you for your invitation, M'sieu Pinaud—I appreciate your consideration.'

M. Pinaud stood up.

'Not at all. May I add to my good-night that I would like you to know how much I envy you.'

*　　*　　*

It was more than a meal. It was a poem.

There were only three other couples dining. M. Pinaud had the fourth corner table and a quarter of the room to himself. Mme Marceau, with the aid of one young girl, took a pride in seeing that no one had to wait for anything.

There were river trout to start, baked in butter and almonds. Then there was an escalope of veal in a white sauce, so tender he could have carved the meat with his fork. The spinach was buttered, the *croquette* potatoes browned to perfection.

M. Marceau appeared just before the trout, carrying a well-laden tray which he set down on the sideboard. He took a different bottle of wine to each one of the three couples in succession, opening it with a lightning dexterity, pouring, and waiting for the inevitable approval with an attention that was always concerned but never deferential.

When he had finished he went back to the sideboard and brought the only decanter from his tray to M. Pinaud's table. It contained at least a litre of white wine.

'You did not order, M'sieu Pinaud,' he said gravely. The tinge of reproach in his voice was so faint as to be hardly discernible. 'And as you were fully occupied with your guest I did not feel justified in disturbing you. I therefore took the liberty of drawing you some of my brother's locally pressed wine, which I have no hesitation in recommending unreservedly.'

He lifted the glass stopper from the decanter and poured a little of the wine into the glass.

'That is not only very kind and thoughtful of you,' M. Pinaud told him politely, 'but also extremely sensible. You are quite right. I was too busy. I have enough on my mind.'

He took the glass and tasted the wine, fully expecting some mediocre local vintage. Serve you right, Pinaud, he thought, for neglecting to pay sufficient attention to a matter of such importance.

Then his eyes opened wide in astonishment. Only once in his life had he drunk anything comparable, and that was an open *Neûchatel* in Switzerland. This was, almost impossibly, even stronger.

'Magnificent,' he whispered reverently.

The wide and loose-lipped mouth split into a happy smile. The resultant effect caused the landlord to look like a grinning satyr.

'I knew you would like it,' he said, filling the glass and placing the decanter on the table. 'I will bring you the red later. It is even better. And considerably stronger.'

As soon as he had gone the trout appeared. M. Pinaud ate and drank—oblivious of the whole world—in a private seventh heaven of delight.

Mme Marceau came to his table with a hot dish in her hands.

'One of the ladies has a very small appetite,' she told him very seriously. 'This I consider to be lamentable. There are just two left, M'sieu Pinaud. And as you can see they are only small. Far too small to keep. And warmed up they lose. They lose definitely.'

Without waiting for an answer, she placed them on his plate.

'Thank you, madame. They are far too delicious to refuse.'

She smiled with genuine pleasure.

'How kind of you. And thank you for the compliment. There is no hurry. Your veal is being kept hot. And this will give me a chance to serve the others.'

Fortified and encouraged by some more of that remarkable wine, he continued to eat trout with undiminished vigour.

The veal, when it came, was exquisitely tender and succulent, the sauce unbelievable. The portion was so generous that he did not need the young girl's encouraging smile and invitation to help himself to more and more vegetables from her tray of dishes, if only to ensure that none of it would be eaten unaccompanied.

Without hurry, in an ordered and tranquil sequence, came a large portion of open apple-tart, covered with a mountain of whipped-cream.

M. Marceau followed it in, carrying the decanter of red wine with a pride that at the moment only he knew was justified. His expression altered magically to one of grave concern as he noticed that—in spite of M. Pinaud's thirst and appreciation—there was still a small quantity of white wine remaining.

'You are undoubtedly right, m'sieu,' he said gravely. 'My brother would be pleased with you. This white is a wine to be drunk with respect and consideration. There is no hurry. I will leave you to pour the red yourself—at your convenience. Believe me, you will need it all with the cheese.'

He placed a clean glass beside the decanter, which was exactly the same size as the previous one, and left the room.

After such a speech, those of M. Pinaud's readers who appreciate his vivid imagination will have no difficulty in understanding how it was that he could almost hear the axe grinding as his host went out.

Possibly, Pinaud, that worthy addressed himself philosophically and reflectively, it may be that you are dreaming and will shortly wake up. It could happen. On the other hand, it is a merciful and comforting thought that such a thing is highly unlikely. Because if it were a dream you would not be worrying about anything but just eating and drinking and enjoying it.

Whereas now there is just the first very faint beginnings of a certain constriction about your waist. Which would never happen in a dream. It would perhaps be advisable to reach up unobtrusively underneath your table-napkin and undo the top button of your trousers . . .

Which he did, and immediately felt better. With his doubts removed, he could now concentrate, with due solemnity, on finishing that amazing white wine. It was perfectly certain that neither M. Marceau nor his wife were running their hotel for charitable purposes and therefore two carafes of wine would inevitably appear on the bill. Whatever the opinions or comments of M. le Chef might be next week, it would be a pity to waste any of it.

Each table had its own cheese-board. His, when it appeared after the dessert as he had asked, was the largest he had ever seen, its surface completely covered by at least twelve different varieties of cheese. There was even a flat round wooden box, which, when he lifted the lid, revealed a Swiss *vacherin*, which was something he had not seen nor eaten for a long time.

Before cutting the long thin loaf, he deliberately sliced a large wedge of Brie and ate it alone.

Then he was ready to pour the red wine. The landlord had been right. It was, if such a thing were possible, even stronger and better than the white.

He emptied his glass in an ecstasy of delight, swiftly refilled it, cut another and larger slice from the loaf, and settled down to enjoy what he had always maintained to be the best part of any meal.

'There is no need to wish you a good appetite, M'sieu Pinaud,' said Mme Marceau as she came to his table. 'That— it is obvious—you already have. Was everything to your satisfaction?'

'Admirable, madame,' he told her. 'May I congratulate you with perfect truth and very great sincerity and admiration, on the most wonderful meal I have enjoyed for a very long time.'

She smiled with genuine pleasure.

'How very kind of you. I am so glad. Please take your time to finish—as long as you wish. Coffee is served until ten o'clock.'

'Thank you once again, madame.'

From the way he reached for the box of *vacherin* as soon as she had gone, one would have thought that he had not eaten for a week . . .

* * *

If the wine that the brother pressed from his local grapes should have brought him fame and recognition, then—M. Pinaud thought—the liqueur that he distilled from his plums deserved not only gold medals but an Emperor's accolade.

It stood on the table before him in a clear glass bottle, the table-lamp reflecting the deep richness of its wondrous green colour. Its taste was even better, and when the scaldingly hot black coffee followed it down his digestive tract he could have sworn that he tasted the flavour of gently simmering plums . . .

Enough, Pinaud, he told himself sternly—after his third glass of this *pruneau* and his third cup of coffee—enough— you are getting fanciful and poetic. It is time you went to bed. You have kept these good people up long enough.

He called in the lounge on his way up to thank his host for a memorable meal and to ask for the key to his room.

The loose-lipped mouth split into a knowing grin.

'The room is not locked, m'sieu—the key is in the door. Sometimes these ancient locks can be troublesome. We are glad that you have enjoyed your meal.'

'It was fantastic. Oh—by the way, I would like an early call in the morning. Six o'clock, if you please. Good night, M'sieu Marceau.'

'Right. I will enter it. Good night to you, m'sieu.'

He climbed the wide shallow stairs to the first floor, realizing that he was gripping the banister with considerable force, but justifying his action with the logical and reasonable contention that such an ornate and beautiful piece of carving must surely have been installed there for a purpose.

He removed the wrought-iron key and opened the door. The light was already on in the room.

The giant four-poster bed stood next to the window, magnificent in all its glory of polished serpentine pillars, curtains, frills and canopy.

Henri of Navarre would have been surprised and no doubt pleased—had his spirit been able to accompany M. Pinaud up the stairs—at the sight of its occupant.

Claudine Romand, completely naked, was lying on the white sheet. She smiled happily and moved her legs deliberately. Then she made an obscene gesture with delightful and surprising grace.

'What a time you have been,' she greeted him. 'I thought you would never stop eating.'

8

Now some of his small-minded detractors—and no man can achieve the eminence of the greatest detective in France without creating several—have been heard to insist, loudly and pompously, that obviously—whatever may be stated by the publisher on the printed page—M. Pinaud lost no time in following the example of Henri of Navarre many centuries ago and climbed immediately into the four-poster bed.

They will argue this contention with the blind conviction of the bigoted, ignoring the written word and quoting their various premises in strict order of rotation—first, that she was so very beautiful and passionate—secondly, that she was both eager and willing—thirdly, that she was completely naked—fourthly, that he had undoubtedly consumed enough liquor to dull his inhibitions and inflame his sexual desires—and fifthly and lastly, for the same reason and therefore most importantly, he was hardly likely to boast of such exploits when recounting and dictating his memoirs.

But his chronicler (who is only concerned with the truth) is in the fortunate position of being able to reassure his faithful if microscopic public that this certainly did not happen. And join with them in ignoring those small-minded and carping morons who invariably yap at the heels of greatness.

The truth, as so often happens, was perfectly simple.

In spite of the incontestable fact that he had undoubtedly consumed a considerable amount of alcohol—even by his own tolerant standards—the shock of seeing her there, in his own room and in his own bed, was enough to sober him, completely, immediately and fully.

He looked down at her, not with the ardent lust he would himself have expected from one of his nature, but with pity and sadness and compassion, while his imagination raced uncontrollably in a kaleidoscope of vivid and poignant images.

His eyes saw, not the slim white form on the bed, but the body of his wife on their wedding night. He imagined, not the carnal act it would be so easy and so delightful to perform with her, but his own feelings and emotions had his own young daughters been degraded and debauched in the same way. And he sighed at the pity and the horror and the shame of it all . . .

When he spoke his voice was curt and incisive, but not unkind.

'Get your clothes on at once. I am taking you home.'

She laughed. In her laughter there was a wild and frenzied abandon that made him shudder.

'Don't be a fool. I did not come here for that.'

He took two swift steps forward and slapped her face.

'Get dressed. You heard what I said. Now. At once.'

136

This time there was a coldness and a menace in his voice that was more frightening to her even than the blow.

Wordlessly she sat up, swung her legs over the side of the bed and reached for her clothes on the chair.

He turned his back and stared out of the window at the dark and sleeping countryside, his powerful hands clenching and opening spasmodically at his sides. This was the first time in his life that he had ever struck a woman.

He felt sick and remorseful, and disgusted with this town of Vallorme and this case of murder he had so eagerly and confidently undertaken to solve.

'I am ready now.'

Her voice was quiet and subdued.

He turned, took her hand and led her out of the room and down the stairs.

'I am taking Mlle Romand home,' he said curtly as he passed the lounge bar, without even looking at the gaping landlord. 'Leave the front door on the latch and I will close and bolt it when I come back.'

He had decided already not to take his car. There was no knowing what she might do while his attention was occupied with driving.

He walked briskly, cold and tense in the cool night air, and did not release her hand until he had knocked on the white-panelled door of her home.

He only spoke to her once as they walked together down the hill and over the bridge, and at the kindness and compassion in his voice the girl caught her breath with emotion.

'I am sorry I had to do that. But this is no life you are leading. This is a madness without a future. You must see Dr Justeron in the morning. He will be able to help.'

She did not answer.

A light was switched on and her mother opened the door.

'I have brought Claudine home,' he said quietly.

'You are kind, M'sieu Pinaud,' she replied gravely. She did not smile. And he noticed that for the first time she did not look at him directly.

'It is getting late,' he told her. 'I would suggest she goes to bed with a hot drink.'

'Yes, Mother,' said Claudine. 'I will do that. I am very tired.'

She stepped inside the room, and then stopped and turned.

'Thank you, M'sieu Pinaud,' she said, very quietly and sincerely.

'There is no need to thank me,' he told her. 'Try to remember what I said.'

'I will bring up your hot milk,' said Mme Romand. 'Please come inside for a moment, M'sieu Pinaud, if only to enable me to thank you.'

He followed them inside and closed the front door behind him. Claudine went straight upstairs. He accompanied Mme Romand into the kitchen.

'If you have a sedative,' he told her, 'I would put a good dose into the milk.'

'Of course. I was going to do that.'

She opened the larder door and took out a bottle of white wine. In the table-drawer she found a corkscrew. Out of the cupboard came two glasses.

'Please sit down and help yourself,' she told him. 'If you do not mind having it in the kitchen here with me while I heat the milk.'

'Of course not. Thank you very much.'

He opened the bottle, poured two glasses of wine and waited courteously until the milk had been heated, the sedative added and the tray taken upstairs.

When she came down, he stood up, drew a chair to the table and waited until she had sat down. Then he placed one glass in front of her.

'Thank you.'

She drank eagerly and set the glass down.

'We do not give toasts anymore in this unhappy house, M'sieu Pinaud. Tell me what you think of this wine. Marceau sells it at the Crown far too soon, far too young—out of the cask. We keep it here in bottles for two years.'

He drank some slowly. It was even stronger and richer than the one he had consumed in the hotel from the carafe. Finding this incredible fact almost impossible to believe, he drank some more, if only to convince himself that the impossible could happen.

'You are quite right,' he told her. 'I thought his was an amazingly good wine—an extraordinary wine—but this—this is unbelievable—impossible—'

For the first time that evening she looked at him directly as she interrupted him.

'And here we are, sitting in the kitchen, and talking about wine.'

Then the tears came, suddenly and blindingly, and she covered her face with her hands in a gesture that was poignant in its hopelessness.

He pulled a clean handkerchief swiftly from his breast-pocket and gently placed one corner between her outspread fingers. Then he took the bottle and refilled their glasses. He did not speak. His very silence seemed to reach out to touch her with gentleness and tolerance, sympathy and understanding.

She used the handkerchief to dry her eyes and again they met his directly and frankly.

'Tell me what happened,' she whispered.

'You know—how she is?'

'Yes. We all know.'

He drank a little more of his wine and then continued, choosing his words very carefully.

'Claudine was in my bed at the hotel when I went upstairs tonight. Marceau will have a few questions to answer in the morning. This is the second time today. The first was here in this house, when you had gone to see Father Lafarge.'

'I did not know that. I did not dream—I can only say that I am sorry. But I do not hold her responsible.'

'Nor do I. But many others would. I spoke to Louis Brevin this evening. He said that Dr Justeron believes she can be treated and cured—'

'Yes—yes—I have spoken to him,' she interrupted eagerly. 'It is all arranged. There is a psychological clinic—'

'Then you must get her there in the morning without fail. Get him to call here if he can and take her. This is vitally important.'

'I know. You do not have to tell me. I am her mother. Help yourself to more wine, M'sieu Pinaud. There is plenty more.'

He refilled their glasses. The bottle was now empty. She stood up at once and went to the larder.

'No—no—I have had enough—' he began.

'Nonsense. It is a good wine and therefore well worth drinking. And this is the only way I can show my gratitude to you.'

She placed another bottle on the table in front of him and sat down again.

'The treatment will cost a fortune, but I am quite prepared to sell this house, if necessary, to pay for it.'

'You must love her very greatly.'

'Of course. I am her mother.'

And then she used the same words as Louis Brevin.

'There is only one way to love, M'sieu Pinaud. I would do anything for that child. I only married him to give her a home. This morning I thought that my troubles were over. Now I understand how his evil is living on after him.'

The tears came to her eyes.

'You must forgive me, M'sieu Pinaud. I am too upset to talk. Thank you for your handkerchief—I will wash and iron it and return it to you tomorrow. If you come then, I will tell you more about her. You deserve an explanation— you have been so kind.'

He stood up at once.

'Of course. But that is not necessary—you have enough to do. I am sorry to have kept you so late.'

She stood up beside him.

'You had every right—since you brought her home. Another glass of wine before you go?'

'No, thank you. It was most enjoyable. I will call in tomorrow—but please do not trouble with the handkerchief.'

She tried bravely to smile.

'Of course I will.'

She walked with him to the front door and said good night.

The night was dark, the moon and stars obscured by low flying clouds. Street-lamps were still on in the High Street of the town, but their numbers were few and far between.

He heard the car start up somewhere behind him as he walked past the last one down the hill towards the ancient stone bridge that spanned the river.

His mind was preoccupied with thought, re-living in its imagination all the confusing and inexplicable things that had happened since the morning. This was a strange town, and the people in it were even stranger. There were under-currents of emotion, tension and secrecy he found hard to understand. In many ways these characters reacted quite differently from what he would have expected. In many ways—

It was at this exact moment that he gave up thinking.

As a vague and unheeded background to his thoughts, he had heard the car accelerating from behind to pass him, but—preoccupied with his own thinking—he had not even bothered to turn around and look. He remembered after-wards, in retrospect, wondering subconsciously and automatically why he had not by now been bathed in the radiance of headlights.

Now, as he came to the low stone parapet of the bridge, the whole world seemed suddenly filled with the roar of the still furiously accelerating engine, and he swung around in the first frantic clutch of fear.

Then three things happened simultaneously.

The headlights suddenly blazed, dazzling and blinding him, tyres screamed as the brakes were jammed hard on, and the car—or rather from his point of view, that blaze of terrifying and blinding light—continued to flash straight towards him where he stood, helpless and vulnerable, at the narrow entrance to the low and medieval bridge.

There was only just room for one car to pass at the time between the huge hand-carved blocks of stone. But with the road sloping steeply down to the river from either side, there were no traffic problems and therefore no signs.

The French motorist is usually—and always has been a profound realist. One saw if another car were approaching, made up one's mind whether to accelerate or to brake, and was still in the happy position of being able to observe if one's decision had been correct or wrong and yet have enough time to change or modify tactics effectively should the oncoming driver happen to be a bloody-minded bastard.

It was really quite simple. Heavy lorries were prohibited from using the bridge. As a historical monument of unique interest, it rated a higher priority than any economic schedule. Signs directed its defeated rivals to the new and massive edifice of steel girders that spanned the river ten kilometres nearer the coast.

His mind raced with the instantaneous wonder of thought.

Only just room for one car to pass at the time. Which meant—since this bloody fool had left it far too late to brake—that he would be crushed and mangled against these old and venerable stones, whose resistance was undoubtedly greater, since they had endured for some nine hundred years, than the flesh and bone which comprised his body . . .

The blind instinct of self-preservation saved his life. As he thought, his muscular reflexes responded instantaneously.

He placed one hand on the parapet and without a second's hesitation hurled himself over the stones and into the river.

The shock was intense. The water was ice-cold from the mountain springs and the current swift and dangerous.

But at least, he thought as his head came up to the surface—at least I am still alive. And one day I will catch that bastard.

For a few seconds he trod water, paddling against the pull of the current, and looked back at the bridge. He saw the rear lights of the car climbing the hill. The headlights had been extinguished. A gust of wind drove the last cloud across the moon. For a moment the back of the car looked familiar, but he could not think why.

Then he swallowed a large mouthful of ice-cold water, and concentrated on the urgent and difficult business of swimming to the bank. Midnight bathing, he reflected ruefully, was hardly an appropriate way in which to conclude the kind of day he had been forced to endure.

A few powerful strokes brought him to the bank. The river was deep and rapid, but not very wide. He scrambled up the steep slope to regain the road and walked up the hill to the hotel as fast as he could, despite the discomfort of his sodden boots and dripping clothes, for by now he was beginning to shiver.

The front door was on the latch. He closed and bolted it behind him. A small light had been left on at the end of the reception counter, but there was no one about. He found the switch and turned it off and then made his way quietly up the stairs to his bedroom in the dark.

There he switched on the light, found his pyjamas, took off his boots and carried them straight into the bathroom without delay.

There was an electric fire which he switched on, a chair which he drew up in front of it and a large bath on four ornate legs which he proceeded to fill almost to the taps with boiling hot water. Then he placed his boots on their sides on the seat of the chair, removed his clothes, wrung them out with all the strength in his powerful hands and arms, and hung and draped them over its back. By this time the bathroom was full of steam, so he had to open the window for a few moments to clear the air.

Then at last he was able to relax. The water was delightfully hot and exquisitely soothing.

Typically, his first thoughts were as to how M. le Chef would react when he came across a claim for a new suit on the expense-sheet of one of his most junior operatives. There was bound to be a terrifying interview, during which he would have to explain and justify both his temerity and his figures.

The amount of the hotel bill alone would almost certainly raise his blood-pressure—for a meal such as he had eaten would inevitably be astronomically in excess of any subsistence allowance ever computed by any government accountant.

To claim a new suit in addition might well induce a stroke. He could argue the case of the hotel bill without difficulty. This was the only hotel in Vallorme, in which town he was trying to solve a murder which he did not believe to be an accident, but the matter of the suit might well be more difficult. Then he had a bright idea. He would wear it for the interview. He looked at the back of the chair. As a suit it no longer qualified.

There was another electric fire in the bedroom. He would have to leave it on for the few hours that were left of the night—since he had to get up early to see Dumont—and continue the treatment with another chair, or else he would never be able to wear it.

He had always preferred to travel light—shirts, underclothes, pyjamas and toilet kit in one suitcase. Perhaps he had been wrong. Perhaps he ought always to take a spare suit. There was no doubt that he was not engaged in a peaceful trade . . .

And then—such is the wonder of thought and the association of ideas—his mind seemed to fly back logically to what had just happened and suddenly he knew why the outlines of the back of the car had seemed familiar.

It was hardly surprising. They were exactly the same as his own.

David Marbon, the young traveller, had told him that he had the same make of car, but not the new model. Body styles, in those days, did not change every year. Improvements and modifications were more important to the engine and chassis.

He dropped the soap and clutched the sides of the bath, tense and ready for action, his weariness forgotten.

Then, even as he tensed, he remembered and relaxed. The car had continued up the hill, away from the town. Even if he called at the house, he would find only the wife and children at home. It would be a waste of time.

David Marbon by now was a long way away—if he had any sense—busily engaged in establishing an alibi to prove that he could not possibly have been anywhere near the bridge at the time when someone else had obviously been confused with him. After all, there were several thousands of that particular make of car on the roads.

He sighed heavily and searched in the water, which by now was opaque, for the soap. Then he applied himself assiduously to the task in hand, which was getting himself clean and dry and warm enough to go to bed. Tomorrow would be time enough to deal with David Marbon.

It had been a long and hard day. It would be nice to sleep. He hoped that by now—with the passing of the years—a mattress would have replaced the herbs and goose-feathers on which Henri of Navarre had once laid his royal limbs.

But it did not really matter, he reflected philosophically as he heaved himself out of the bath and began to apply the towel vigorously. He was so tired that he was sure to sleep, even if they had left the original bedding in order to add even more historical interest to their antique and valuable bed.

Yet before he slept—tired as he was—he remembered to say a prayer to thank the good God Who with infinite mercy had saved his life.

9

He slept profoundly and dreamlessly for the few remaining hours of the night, which was hardly surprising.

At the gentle but persistent knocking on the door he awoke like a giant refreshed and called out: 'Come in' with hearty cheerfulness.

It was Mme Marceau herself who brought in a tray with coffee and *croissants* and set it down on a chair beside the bed.

'Good morning, M'sieu Pinaud. You asked for an early call. It is six o'clock.'

She seemed strangely quiet and subdued this morning, quite unlike her usual self. This was a different woman. Her eyes looked once at him as she came in, and then everywhere except at the bed.

If she deplored the extreme temperature of her best bedroom, in spite of the window he had left open all night, or if she considered the habit of spreading out articles of clothing all over the furniture to be one customary in the big city from whence he came, he would never know. She made no comment.

'Thank you very much, madame,' he said politely. She inclined her head in acknowledgement, but did not answer. At the door she paused and turned.

'Will you be in for lunch, m'sieu? We serve it at midday.'

It was a routine question, but even so he could tell that she had not the slightest interest in his answer. He tried to penetrate the barrier between them.

'After the memorable experience of that exquisite dinner last night,' he told her, speaking deliberately with warmth and sincerity, 'I shall make a point of being here, whatever I am doing, at midday.'

'Thank you, m'sieu.'

The words were flat, disinterested and empty, without warmth or meaning. The door opened and closed, and she was gone.

Surely she could not have had anything to do with the previous occupant of this beautiful bed, he reflected as he poured himself what was always the best cup of coffee of the day. That was far more likely to have had the connivance of her loose-lipped husband, if there was any truth in the old saying that character can be read in features. He would make a point of seeing that one later and finding out the truth.

By the time he had finished eating and drinking, washed and shaved, and pulled and tugged and strained and stretched in a vain effort to restore some shape into what had once been a perfectly good suit, he realized that he would have to take his car, or else he would be late for Ulysse Dumont. He could drive it to the cottage and then walk into the wood.

His car started at the first touch of the starter, which was only to be expected as a result of the conscientious way in which he always looked after it. He wound his window down to its fullest extent. There was an autumn chill in the early-morning air, but he still felt warm after a night spent in company with his drying clothes.

He drove carefully out of the car-park on to the road and then accelerated down the hill towards the bridge.

Ahead of him, crossing it, he recognized the figure of Louis Brevin and his dog Nero, walking in the same direction. The oncoming road was clear, but his foot was already on the brake, since the bridge was narrow and he estimated that they would not have reached the other side by the time he was on it.

Through the open window he heard a short sharp whistle.

Immediately—and with incredible speed—the dog turned and bounded back in great leaps across the bridge towards him.

His reflexes acted instinctively. He was practically at the bridge, the dog still on it, right in front of him. There was only one thing to be done. He jammed on the brakes with all his strength and turned the wheel hard to the right to avoid the dog.

The tyres screamed as the wheels locked, and the momentum of the car carried the near front side with a sickening crash into the first stones of the parapet. There could be no doubt as to which material had triumphed in the encounter.

Nero stopped, wagging his tail. Brevin re-crossed the bridge at a run and came to stand by the open window.

'Are you all right?' he asked anxiously.

The engine was still running. M. Pinaud switched it off, opened the door and got out. He was both shaken and furious. Quite apart from the damage to his beloved car, at which he felt like weeping, this idiocy would make him late for his appointment with Dumont.

He ignored the question and walked round the back of the car to examine the damage. It was extensive enough, but mainly confined to the bodywork. His speed had not been great enough at the time of impact to anticipate damage to the wheel adjustment or the chassis. Then he walked back to Brevin.

'I heard a whistle,' he said. His voice was cold and accusing, his eyes hard.

The young man was contrite and apologetic.

'I know—I am terribly sorry. I can't think what made him do it. I heard the car coming. You seemed to be driving rather fast. I did not even trouble to turn. I just whistled to him to go on ahead to give you more room.'

M. Pinaud continued to look at him. Neither his voice nor the expression in his eyes changed.

'That is a perfectly reasonable and logical explanation. Unfortunately I do not believe a word of it. You are not going to stand there and tell me and expect me to accept that an intelligent dog like Nero, whom you have trained yourself, hears your whistle and does something different.'

Brevin's eyes were apprehensive. M. Pinaud in this mood could be terrifying. But their regard did not waver nor falter as they continued to meet that hard accusing stare frankly, and with and behind the fear M. Pinaud could recognize a great courage.

'I am sorry you do not believe me,' he said quietly.

'But this is what happened. Dogs can be as unpredictable as human beings.'

There was a long silence. M. Pinaud contemplated him thoughtfully. They stood there alone on the bridge, while an unseen sun began to warm the chill from the morning air. It was still too early for the local traffic.

A bird sang, tentatively at first, and then suddenly, boldly and exquisitely, from a nearby tree on the river bank.

Nero, after his efforts, had been panting with a lolling tongue. Now he sat down, licking his chops, quite prepared to wait.

'You love that dog very greatly, do you not, M'sieu Brevin?'

His voice now was completely different, quiet and conversational, the cold eyes no longer hostile, but dark with concentration and thought.

'Yes—I do.'

'And yet you were prepared to risk his life just now. You did not know how I could drive or what I would do. Some men would have steered straight at him rather than damage their cars.'

A quick and sudden smile transfigured the anxious brooding lines of Brevin's features.

'Not you,' he replied immediately. And then in the same breath he added:

'I am sorry you do not believe me, M'sieu Pinaud.'

'I find it quite impossible to do that. But there is nothing to be done. I have no proof. It is your word against mine.'

Then suddenly he too smiled.

'And Nero is not going to talk, is he?'

He held out his hand.

153

'Good-bye, M'sieu Brevin. You took a great risk. I can only hope that your motive was worthy of it.'

Wondering, the young man clasped his hand.

'But—but is there anything I can do? Your car—'

'The damage seems to have been mainly to the body-work,' M. Pinaud interrupted him. 'I slowed up when I saw you. But thank you for your offer. I shall take it now to the garage and have an expert opinion.'

He started the car, let in the clutch, reversed away from the parapet and then drove away.

'Well now,' said Jean Latour cheerfully, replacing the buckled bonnet in approximately its normal place with the aid of a hammer and a tyre-lever. 'I would say that you only need a new bonnet, a near-side headlight, new front wing and side-light, new fender, new wing-mirror, new running-board—and all the dents, bruises and scratches removed from the front door panel with re-spraying. You are lucky your radiator escaped—only because this is the one manufacturer who has the good sense to put it behind the engine to protect it.'

Having concluded this triumphant speech, he then smiled up happily at M. Pinaud's melancholy countenance.

'Again, luckily, you seem to have escaped any kind of basic chassis damage. I have checked your wheel-alignment, stub-axles, springing, steering-linkage and connections, clutch, drive-shaft and the half-shaft drives to the back wheels. You were fortunate. It could have been much worse. Anyone who tries to demolish our bridge with an automobile usually pays the penalty.'

He wiped his hands, which still looked immaculately clean, on an even cleaner piece of rag and continued to speak with unabated eloquence.

'I can do all this for you if you wish—provided you give me time—and make a good job of it too. But no doubt you will prefer to go back to Paris, where your insurance company will pay some gang of thieves three times what I would charge you, and so everyone will be happy. You are indeed lucky—this car will still take you there without any trouble, provided you drive in daylight.'

M. Pinaud thanked him politely and felt for his notecase.

'You are very kind,' he said. 'I am fortunate in having the advice of such an expert. I would have liked you to do the work, but I think I had better try to get back in daylight today or tomorrow if possible. I do not own this car, and therefore it will save a good deal of complication if my chief claims on the insurance and allows them to allocate the repairs to one of the garages on their list.

'As you so rightly say, they are bound to overcharge and I am sure that you would make a better job of it, but you must understand that the matter is now completely out of my hands. Now—how much do I owe you?'

'There is no charge, m'sieu.'

'What do you mean?'

Latour looked at him directly and frankly.

'There is no charge because I have done nothing, m'sieu. I only examined your car and have given you my opinion. I do not charge unless I have worked.'

'But your time—'

'It was not very long.'

155

Suddenly the bold and humorous face became grave and intense.

'Besides—we are all fond of Nero here, m'sieu. There is a dog and a half for you. I heard what you did at the bridge. I do not charge a man who prefers to wreck his car rather than kill a dog.'

M. Pinaud replaced his notecase very thoughtfully. This was indeed a strange town, with some very strange people in it. Someone had told him quite recently that everyone in it knew what everyone else was doing. He could not remember who it was—there were so many other things crowding into his mind at the moment.

But it did not matter. The sooner he got to Ulysse Dumont at his tree-felling the better. This stupid business had already delayed him so much that it was quite likely he would not even be there.

But he had to try. For this he was paid. Inadequately, it was true. But that was a matter of argument. Having accepted the wage, there was an obligation upon him which it was unthinkable to one of his character that he should not honour.

He smiled and held out his hand.

'Thank you,' he said, and although his voice was quiet, it was moving with a great sincerity. 'Both for your help and for what you have just said. I am honoured to shake your hand.'

Latour's clasp was strong and sure.

'The privilege is mine,' he replied. 'I wish you a good and safe journey home.'

'Thank you.'

As M. Pinaud drove out of the forecourt, he saw Latour, in his driving-mirror, walking quickly towards the telephone-box.

*   *   *

He left his car in front of the cottage, got out and walked down a narrow lane towards the forest at the back.

Guided by the distant high-pitched whine of a mechanical saw, he turned to the left where a second path crossed the first at right angles, directing his steps towards the sound.

He came nearer and nearer, the sound increasing in volume with every step he took. Then, suddenly, it ceased, but before he could appreciate the vast silence it had left, he heard the singing shout that woodsmen have given since time immemorial in every country in the world:

'Tim—ber—'

That bellowing and resonant voice was unmistakable.

He looked up at once, alert and tense, and seemed to freeze in horror for one second as he saw the great tall tree falling in front of him, at first with majestic and deceptive slowness, to the accompaniment of rending and cracking wood and snapping and splitting bark—directly and appallingly straight down in front of him, as if crashing out of the very gate of heaven to crush into oblivion the whole world and everyone in it below . . .

For that one second the terrifying horror of the imminent threat seemed to paralyse him. Then the basic instinct of self-preservation galvanized his reflexes to contract, tense and activate every muscle in his body.

That same upward glance which had so shocked him indicated the direction of the fall.

In one great leap he hurled himself to the side, sprawled on the ground, rolled over in the same movement, using the momentum of his leap to add to the distance—and finished on his hands and knees, crawling and clutching through the undergrowth in desperate and frantic haste away from that horrifying nightmare descending upon him. He looked up at that great surging trunk and its branches—immense in their towering height and endless spread—sweeping down, now with incredible speed, from the clear light of the morning sky. They seemed to fall faster and faster, inevitably and relentlessly, down to the dim and shadowed horror of the undergrowth all around him in which he was groping worm-like for his life.

But there could be no dignity in trying to escape from death. What was dignity—what was it worth—what could it mean—compared to the precious gift of life?

Mocking his panic—like a cry not from above but from the very underworld in which he lay—he heard it again:

'Tim—ber—'

With each metre of fall the frightening speed increased. All the time he fought desperately to get away—to get clear— to save his life.

Then—with a crash like the thunder of the last trump—the tree hit the earth.

He felt an agonizing pain as the side shoot of a massive branch hit his outstretched arm. Mercifully, the rest of it smashed down into the wet leaves beside him.

And then there was silence—utter, complete and universal silence. There was no longer the screaming whine of the mechanical saw. There was no more futile and inane shouting of warning when it was too late to do anything about it. There was no cracking and splintering of wood that had grown and matured with grace and beauty and dignity for centuries, only to be torn and tortured and destroyed by man.

There was nothing, except a great and peaceful and wonderful silence, in which he relaxed and gave thanks to the good God, with humility and thankfulness, that he was still alive . . .

Then he rose slowly to his feet, stripped off his jacket, rolled up his sleeve and felt his forearm.

The bone was not broken, but the flesh was blue and swollen. Tendons and muscles must have been severely bruised. He would have to see Dr Justeron quickly and get it strapped up, or else he would never be able to drive home.

He rolled down the sleeve, put on his jacket and began to walk towards the base of the tree. It had fallen along the line of the path on which he had been walking. He must have rolled and crawled quite a long way, he thought. But then it had been a large and tall tree.

Towards him, approaching from the other side, came the burly figure of Ulysse Dumont. There was no haste in his approach, but he was walking deliberately, like a man with a mission.

He reached one side of the massive trunk as M. Pinaud came to the other. For a moment they eyed each other across it, each man tense, alert and watchful. There was a menace in that short and immensely powerful figure which made M. Pinaud thankful that he had not buttoned his jacket. He breathed in deeply and inflated his chest. The butt of his revolver in its shoulder-holster was now free and available.

'Are you all right, M'sieu Pinaud?'

The question was neither urgent nor anxious in the way that Louis Brevin had spoken. He might have been asking about the weather.

'My arm is rather badly bruised. I shall have to go to Dr Justeron. But I escaped. No thanks to you.'

Reaction had now set in, and to his intense annoyance M. Pinaud found that he was actually trembling. He clenched his hands at his sides as he spoke, ignoring the stabbing pain that shot up his forearm.

'What do you mean by that?'

'I mean, M'sieu Dumont, that a man whose family have been woodsmen for generations would have known exactly as to how, when and where that tree would fall.'

He was both angry and upset, and most of his emotion was clearly expressed in the tone of his voice.

But Dumont ignored it. His own was calm as he replied.

'Of course I did. My pride in myself, my family and my trade would never permit me to deny such a statement. Observe the line of this trunk. Exactly parallel with the edges of this path. Precisely where I calculated. Which makes it so much easier to cart away the logs once they have been sawn.'

'Then why shout your warning too late?'

'I do not understand—'

'It is not difficult. You must have seen me coming down the path.'

This statement, which M. Pinaud considered reasonable

enough in view of what he had been compelled to endure, let loose a veritable torrent of words in a flood of eloquence.

'Of course I did not see you. How could I have seen you when I was not even looking? If I had seen you I would have shouted in time to warn you. I am not an idiot. But neither am I clairvoyant. Nor am I gifted with telescopic sight.

'I shouted from sheer habit. I shouted because we have always shouted since the beginning of time. I shouted because I always shout when the mass gives with the weight and the split widens. Naturally I did not see you for the simple reason that I was not even looking for you. I was watching something far more important—the blade of my saw. You sometimes get a stone embedded in a trunk, with the bark at the base grown around it.

'I said seven o'clock. You yourself agreed to be here at seven o'clock. Those were your last words as you left my woodshed. I gave you up long ago and began sawing. Look at your watch now, M'sieu Pinaud, and tell me the time.'

Here he paused through sheer lack of breath.

'Then why did you ask if I was all right? Were you expecting me to be hurt or killed?'

M. Pinaud's voice was calmer and quieter now. He was rapidly regaining control of himself once more. He unclenched his hands as he spoke.

He waited patiently while Dumont took in several more deep breaths to replenish his exhausted lungs. Then once again that great resonant voice rent and sundered the sleeping silence of the forest.

'Of course I did. Of course I was. Anyone who walks in this forest when Ulysse Dumont is felling trees can well expect to be hurt or killed. That is why I shout. That is what I told you before. When I came along here to check the line of the fall I saw you walking and knew that you must have been in danger. That is why I asked.'

M. Pinaud sighed. It was obvious that he was not making a great deal of progress. This individual was a hard one and tough one.

'It was an accident, then?' he asked quietly.

The deep-set humorous eyes narrowed and appraised him shrewdly, calculatingly and defiantly.

'Yes, m'sieu. An accident—just like the accident which befell Colonel Romand.'

For a long moment there was silence. To M. Pinaud it seemed sinister and threatening, filled with the menace of the lie that had been so aggressively and so defiantly uttered. The challenge had been explicitly stated. His meaning was clear.

Then M. Pinaud buttoned his jacket and was turning to go when Dumont spoke again.

'Did you wish to ask me some questions, M'sieu Pinaud?'

In his voice as he said this there was nothing of the defiance that had hardened it before and glinted in his eyes. It was reasonably modulated, completely respectful and without any other expression.

M. Pinaud regarded him thoughtfully, and then chose his words with care.

'I did,' he replied. 'But now I have decided that it would almost certainly be a waste of time. And time is the one thing in my life of which I have never found enough. There are always so many things to be done, and so little time in which to do them. I wish you good-day, M'sieu Dumont.'

He turned his back without waiting for a reply and began skirting the wide-spreading branches of the fallen tree to regain the path that would lead him back to his car.

He sat behind the wheel for some time, thinking, ignoring the pain in his throbbing arm. Dumont's words had given him enough to think about.

There had been far too many accidents recently in this town of Vallorme. Last night he had nearly been run over and forced to jump into the river. This morning he had been obliged to wreck his car and—had he been driving faster— could easily have ended up in hospital. And just now in the forest he had been warned too late and was fortunate in being able to sit in his car. He might have been lying under the trunk or one of those massive branches of that fallen tree.

But Dumont had been the first to link together what might well have been cause and effect. Were these accidents happening to him because he so steadfastly refused to believe that one had happened to Colonel Romand?

In that case there had been both cause and effects. The effects had been plain and apparent, but the cause was more difficult.

How was it that these three different men, all leading separate and diverse lives, all of whom were suspects in that they were bound together by a common hatred of the murdered man, could have conspired together in this way so effectively against him? If there had been complicity, who was behind it all? Who was organizing it—since organization was manifest?

He did not know. But one thing was certain. He was going to find out.

He sighed profoundly and lit a cigarette. The pain in his arm compelled him to do this one-handed, which turned what should have been a simple task into a major operation.

It did not seem, Pinaud, he told himself in a sudden fit of depression, as though you were making very much progress with this case. If you are, it would appear to be backwards. And what is more, it would seem that you have not finished yet in that direction.

Remember that Dr Justeron is apparently some relation of Mme Romand. He may well be mixed up in all this too. You know what he told you about Colonel Romand. What if he pretends to look after your arm and slyly injects some filthy germ into your bloodstream, telling you cheerfully that it is an antiseptic?

But you have no choice. You will not be able to stand this pain much longer, and he is the only doctor in Vallorme.

And what about your suit? He looked down at his trousers in dismay. Rolling about on the wet and slimy leaves had not only negated all his painstaking efforts of the night before but definitely made the suit look far worse than it had done dripping wet. At least the river water had been comparatively clean.

He sighed again, crushed out his cigarette and started the engine.

10

There were several people, all sitting on the plain wooden chairs beneath the posters on the walls of what had once been the hall of the doctor's gracious town house and was now the waiting-room next door to the surgery.

Through an aperture which had been built into the partition wall a charming young lady in an immaculate white overall raised a glass window swiftly and gave him to understand, very politely, that since he did not have an appointment during surgery hours he would be the first to realize that there was bound to be some slight delay while Dr Justeron attended to those cases which were urgent. Of course, if the pain was unendurable—

M. Pinaud interrupted her cheerfully and assured her that he would be able to endure it until the doctor could find time to attend to him. This earned him a captivating smile and then she went back to her bottles and boxes in what was obviously the dispensary.

The other people had looked up as he entered, vouchsafed him a civil good morning, and then returned without delay to discussing their various ailments with great enthusiasm and a total lack of inhibition.

There were altogether six of them, two ladies and four men. They appeared to have gravitated naturally into couples, one talker with a loud and authoritative voice, and one listener, subdued, sympathetic and duly impressed.

He sat down and fumbled in his pocket for his cigarettes. Then he realized that the largest and most vivid poster of all on the opposite wall listed and illustrated in prolific detail and with revolting realism all the horrible and terrifying things that smoking could do to his body and his health.

He removed his hand guiltily and composed himself to wait. The voices around him had not ceased after their polite greeting. Regardless of his own wishes, it was impossible, in that confined space, to avoid listening to odd snatches of their conversation, which was so extraordinarily frank and clinical that it completely absorbed his attention until an incredibly old man walked slowly and painfully out through the far door into the waiting-room.

The charming young lady in the white overall raised the glass window and thrust her exquisitely coiffured head through the aperture.

'M'sieu Pinaud—Dr Justeron will see you now.'

She then included all the other people, who somewhat understandably had fallen silent as the window lifted, in the splendid companionship of her comforting and encouraging smile as she continued to speak.

'I am sure all you good people will understand and not mind being patient for a little longer. As you know, a patient in pain has priority. M'sieu Pinaud has had an accident and his arm is very painful. Dr Justeron assures me that the delay will not be long. Thank you for your consideration.'

The window was closed. The waiting patients began to talk again. Now it was the turn of those who had listened so patiently to relate their own experiences.

But these he would never be privileged to share. After what he had just been more or less compelled to hear, perhaps it was just as well . . .

He stood up and walked through the far door into the surgery.

In his own domain Dr Justeron was brisk and competent. He finished washing his hands in a small hand-basin and dried them as he spoke.

'Ah yes, M'sieu Pinaud. Jacket off and sleeve up, if you please, and over on that couch. No—the other way—I want the arm next to me. Thank you.'

He gave his orders in a quiet but authoritative voice, as if he knew that it was not him nor his wishes but his knowledge and experience that were being obeyed.

He took the forearm in his strong and beautiful hands and began to feel it very slowly and carefully.

'And relax,' he continued, without even looking up from his task. 'You are as taut and strung-up as a piano-wire.'

M. Pinaud tried to obey, but could not refrain from retorting:

'And so would you be if you had narrowly escaped death three times in the past twelve hours.'

The doctor did not cease from his meticulous feeling and probing as he replied.

'I dare say. But my advice is still good, just the same. Whatever has happened to you is over. You are now here and in my care.'

He straightened up.

'You are fortunate. No bones broken. I should think the tendons, sinews and one or two muscles are badly bruised. You must have had considerable pain.'

'I did. I still have.'

'I can give you something for that. Both on the arm and some tablets to swallow. Ask for them on your way out.'

He walked over to a cupboard, took out a jar of ointment and with two fingers began smearing it very lightly and delicately over M. Pinaud's forearm. It was soothing and aromatic. The effect was almost magical.

'Then I am going to bind it up, quite tightly, below the elbow. It will only be a short bandage, which will leave your hand and fingers free. But I would advise you to see your own doctor for an X ray as soon as you get back.'

'You mean if I get back.'

The wide and intelligent eyes regarded him calmly.

'No, I do not. I meant what I said. I told you to relax.'

'I know you did. I find it difficult.'

'Obviously. But at the moment I am your doctor and you are my patient, of your own volition, and I flatter myself that I know rather more about the subject under discussion than you do.'

'Granted. But how can I relax?'

'You can try. I told you the last time I saw you to abandon this whole thing and go home. I should imagine that Father Lafarge gave you the same advice.'

'He did. I am not used to being told what to do. I make my own decisions.'

'That is evident.'

'And I find it strange—and not a thought conducive to relaxing—that both you and your charming receptionist seem to know all about me and my pain without my having even to tell you—'

'There is nothing strange about that. Dumont telephoned me before you came here.'

'I see.'

He thought rapidly for a moment. And then all his pent-up emotions burst out in a torrent of words.

'Yet I still find it strange how all the telephones in this town seem to work with such incredible efficiency. I should imagine Jean Latour's sweetheart Yvonne must have been working overtime since I arrived. The liaison work must be comparable to that of the intelligence in an Army Headquarters. How did Louis Brevin know at what exact time to take his dog for a morning walk—of course—there is a telephone in the Crown Hotel. If someone told him about my early call he would have had no difficulty.

'Last night, when I took Claudine home, another telephone-call would have told David Marbon about what time to expect me back from her house, so that he could wait in his car until I had passed and then try to kill me at the bridge.

'The object of Brevin's exercise with his dog was to delay me sufficiently to make me late for my appointment with Dumont, who could then take his turn in what seems to be the fashionable sport these days in Vallorme—that of killing Pinaud—without having it lie unduly on his conscience.

'All the telephones in Vallorme seem to be functioning admirably to keep all its inhabitants fully informed as to what I am doing, except that of Mme Romand, who told me that hers was out of order. That is why I, a complete stranger, had to be told personally of the death of her husband, instead of her simply ringing the police. Unfortunately for all of you in this town, I was the wrong kind of stranger.'

'And a very obstinate one,' the doctor interjected dryly.

'I am Pinaud of the *Sûreté*,' he replied with dignity and pride.

The indulgent reader will surely forgive him for his outburst. He had suffered agonizing pain and the tension of three narrow escapes from what could easily have been death. Dr Justeron had no difficulty in doing the same. A charming smile transfigured his features.

'If it is any consolation to you, I quite agree with everything you have said. But as I told you before, I am now your doctor, you are now in my surgery, and I have told you to relax. Since I am treating you to the best of my not inconsiderable ability, surely it is not unreasonable to expect you to obey me instead of talking so much.'

Then he went to the same cupboard for a bandage. M. Pinaud was duly impressed and suitably subdued.

The ensuing silence lasted some considerable time while the doctor, with swift and impressive competence, continued to bandage his forearm. It was M. Pinaud who eventually broke it.

'I was glad and thankful to hear from her mother,' he said quietly, 'that you think Claudine can be cured.'

The doctor did not look up from his bandaging. His voice as he replied was completely without expression.

'Of course she can. She needs psycho-analysis in a competent clinic, that is all. The girl is a nymphomaniac. This is not her fault, considering that she was born with very strong sexual emotions, inherited from her mother, but due to the fact that these were erotically and unnaturally stimulated at a far too early age by her stepfather, the late Colonel Romand. Now that he is dead, the treatment can begin. I am taking her there myself today, as soon as I have finished surgery.'

Again there was a long silence, through which it seemed to M. Pinaud's vivid imagination that it was as if the words, in some indefinable way, continued to drift down endlessly, implacably, relentlessly, like autumn leaves falling on a windless day, but above all without a sound, even though they had been spoken, as if ashamed of the horror they carried within them . . .

The doctor finished his bandaging and straightened up. As he spoke his voice was again brisk and professional.

'There—that will see you home to Paris. But go to your own doctor as soon as you can.'

M. Pinaud began to roll down his sleeve.

'I will,' he said quietly. 'Thank you very much for all that you have done. It feels better already. The pain has nearly gone.'

Dr Justeron looked at him thoughtfully for what seemed a very long time. When he spoke his voice had changed once more. Now it was warm and compassionate, rich and vibrant with emotion.

171

'Not at all. Thank you, M'sieu Pinaud, for not trying to reply to what I told you just now. There are certain things that some of us here in Vallorme—I am afraid many of us—cannot even bear to discuss.'

He paused for a few seconds, as if to collect his thoughts.

'In the course of my career it has been my desolation, my duty, and sometimes my consolation to watch many people die. Some I have envied—those who had the rare privilege of dying tranquilly and peacefully in bed, surrounded by their families and still able to see the tears in the eyes of those who loved them so deeply.

'Colonel Romand, I am delighted to say, did not have that privilege. He met the death he so richly deserved—shot down like a wild animal from behind. Now do you understand why I asked you to go home?'

M. Pinaud looked at him straight in the eyes, held out his hand and answered the question with one word.

'Yes.'

They shook hands strongly. The doctor waited until he had replaced his jacket and then escorted him to the door. Before he reached it M. Pinaud stopped.

'What do I owe you, Doctor?'

'Nothing.'

'Why not?'

'Because you have done so much already for Mme Romand and Claudine. There is a box for charity in the waiting-room, if you wish.'

'Thank you. I am grateful.'

Dr Justeron opened the door.

'I could not persuade you to go home before, M'sieu Pinaud. I asked you to see Father Lafarge. I am now asking you to do so, once again. If you feel any gratitude please do what I ask.'

M. Pinaud glanced at his watch. He knew that he needed a drink after the experiences of that morning—several drinks—more than he needed anything else just then in the whole world. And he had promised to return to the hotel at twelve o'clock. It was later than he had thought.

'I promise you I will go as soon as I have finished lunch,' he said. 'Good-bye, Dr Justeron, and thank you once again.'

'Is your husband in, madame?'

'No, m'sieu—but he told me to leave the bottle of absinthe out, with the ice and lemon. It is all ready for you on the table there.'

Her manner was still strangely constrained, her voice subdued. Her eyes met his once, and then looked at everything else in the room except him.

'Thank you, madame,' he said politely. 'That was a kind and intelligent thought. When will he be back? I would like to have a few words with him.'

'Oh—he will not be very long. He had to go to see his brother at the vineyard. Lunch is at twelve.'

'I know. That is why I came back.'

She did not answer as she left the room. Wondering at the change in her manner, he sat down and poured himself a generous drink, nodding a civil acknowledgement to the greeting from the two farm-labourers who were busily and solemnly engaged at an adjoining table in apparently seeing who could finish first the enormous carafe of red wine which stood in front of each of them.

The air was thick with acrid blue smoke from their hand-rolled cigarettes. M. Pinaud proceeded to make it even thicker by lighting one of his own.

The absinthe was delicious. He finished his glass, and made another drink and relaxed for the first time that morning.

He felt strangely content, in spite of all that had happened. Perhaps because his arm was no longer hurting him. But he could not help wondering what could have upset Mme Marceau so much.

One of the farm-labourers extracted a worn leather purse from an inner pocket and placed a small coin deliberately on the table in front of his companion, whose carafe and glass were both empty. Then he got up, clumsy in his huge mud-encrusted boots, and walked to the bar, where he rang the bell, smiling cheerfully.

Mme Marceau came in quickly, took down two more carafes from the shelf, and proceeded to fill them both from one of the barrels behind the bar. She did not look at M. Pinaud.

'There will be no betting or gambling in this café, Théophile,' she told him severely.

He looked at her with wide-eyed innocence.

'There never is, madame.'

'I heard the coin on the table.'

'That was a debt, madame, not a bet. Onésime paid my bus-fare last Sunday.'

She finished filling the carafes, counted and took his money and put it in a drawer.

'You have been warned, Théophile,' she said with an even greater severity as she went out.

Théophile carried the two heavy carafes easily in one huge hand back to their table, winking happily at M. Pinaud on the way.

'The one who finishes his first does not pay for the next,' he said. 'It is an old custom here in Vallorme.'

'And a very good one too,' M. Pinaud told him, making himself another drink. 'Your very good health, gentlemen.'

A cheerful growl from the other table acknowledged his politeness.

He looked at his watch. There was just time for one more quick one.

Punctually at one minute to twelve he stood up, replaced his tray on the bar counter and went into the restaurant.

He was the only occupant. His table was laid. Mme Marceau saw him come into the room and brought in his soup immediately. He began to eat his lunch.

The bread was stale, the butter rancid. The soup was lukewarm. After the first two mouthfuls he saw a long black hair appear on the surface.

He pushed his plate away in disgust and rang the bell on the table.

When Mme Marceau appeared, he pointed to the plate.

'I am sorry, madame—but all this is hardly up to your standard. The bread is stale, the butter is rancid, the soup is not even hot and that hair in it does not   '

'I am very sorry, m'sieu—but I have had one of those mornings—the refrigerator has gone wrong and the baker did not even call. Let me bring you some more—'

For the first time, he noticed, she was looking at him directly, and he wondered at the pain and the misery he could see in her eyes.

'No, thank you. I think I have lost my appetite.'

'The chicken will be all right. I will bring it in now.'

The carafe of wine on the table looked exactly the same as the night before. As soon as she had left the room he poured himself out a glass and swallowed a gigantic gulp.

It might have looked the same as that exquisitely flavoured vintage he had enjoyed so much the night before, but definitely it did not taste the same.

With admirable self-restraint he forbore from spitting it out immediately on the floor. It may have been the same colour— but its taste called forth almost simultaneously to his vivid imagination a comparison with the urine of a horse, were anyone misguided enough to attempt to drink such a thing.

The chicken, when it came, was red and underdone. The cabbage was soggy, the potatoes hard.

He pushed his plate away and rang the bell for the second time.

As Mme Marceau came to the table, he gestured wordlessly to where the chicken-leg he had sliced down the middle seemed to stare, redly and accusingly, at both of them.

176

'The wine—' he began.

'I know, m'sieu,' she interrupted breathlessly. 'I am very sorry. There must have been some mix-up—that is why my husband had to go to see his brother. I will bring you some cheese.'

And without waiting for an answer she fled to the kitchen.

Instead of the magnificent cheese-board of the night before, one portion of overripe Gorgonzola was put down in front of him. With it she brought a carafe of red wine and once again rushed out before he could even speak.

He took a knife and cut the cheese eagerly, for by now his gargantuan appetite was beginning to feel the strain of this unending frustration.

Something small and black and slimy crawled out of the cheese with a determined and horrifying deliberation, making purposefully for the edge of the dish in the pursuit of concealment and safety.

With a shudder he dropped the knife and in desperation poured out some of the red wine into a clean glass.

Mercifully, profiting by experience, he had the sense to swallow only a modest mouthful and not a gigantic gulp. It was just as well.

His description of this one was spoken out aloud, since he was alone in the room, but could only be related in after years to his friends and intimates, and never to his chronicler, who although only concerned with the truth, is yet subject to a very rigid censorship.

For a long moment he sat there, thinking. Then he sighed philosophically and lit a cigarette. There is no doubt, Pinaud, he told himself, that you have enjoyed better meals than this one.

Then he made up his mind and rang the bell for the third time.

She came out through the kitchen door, and in one swift and lithe movement he stood up and pulled out the chair next to him.

'Please come here and sit down, madame,' he said, quietly and gently and with kindness, remembering vividly the pain and the misery he had seen in her eyes, 'and be good enough to give me a few moments of your time, even if you are busy.'

His voice was so sympathetic and so compelling that she complied as if in a dream. Her movements were slow and hesitant, as if she were acting against her own will and judgment.

He sat down beside her and began to speak again.

'Last night, madame, I had the privilege of enjoying what was perhaps the most delightful and memorable of all the outstanding meals I have ever eaten in my life. No wonder the Crown Hotel has such a reputation for its *cuisine*. You could easily qualify for a *cordon bleu* chef— you have the necessary touch of genius.'

'Thank you, m'sieu,' she said quietly.

'Which brings me to this.'

One outstretched hand gestured down—with a contempt more eloquent than words—at the table.

'This was not a meal—but a bad joke. Would you be kind enough to tell me why?'

For a long moment there was silence. Then, because his eyes were kind and compassionate, at last she replied.

'They—they thought it might help.'

'Who are they?'

'I promised not to say.'

There was another silence. With that tact and innate understanding which was so much a part of his nature he did not break it.

Then the tears came—quick and merciful and healing— perhaps because of the kindness, tenderness and understanding in his voice—an anodyne, a relief and a comfort to all the emotions she had been concealing and repressing within her for so long.

Still he waited in silence, knowing that now the dam had broken she would surely speak in her own good time.

When the words finally came, they seemed sad and small and separate, like pebbles dropped singly into the depths of some still and silent pool.

'The idea was to stop any arrest you might be thinking of making and to drive you out of town. Not necessarily to kill you—although the risk was always there—but mainly to injure you in some minor and not too serious way and therefore frighten you enough to drive you away from here.'

For the sake of his own self-respect he felt impelled to speak.

'I am not a man who frightens easily,' he said quietly.

'No. That is evident. You have every reason to be proud. You know that you have been under constant su-

pervision ever since you came here yesterday. They know—
and knew— all your movements—'

'But who are they, madame?'

'I told you I promised not to say.'

'And was it their orders that brought Claudine to my bed
last night?'

'No—no—that was entirely her own idea. No one was
told, except my husband, who had to arrange to let her
in—and of course not Louis Brevin, who would have gone
stark raving mad had he known. You see, he still loves
her, and we are all sure he will marry her as soon as Dr
Justeron's treatment has cured her. And then they can
make a new life together.

'But as she is now—we all accepted the fact that there
was no point in arguing with her. She had made up her
mind, and until she is cured I am afraid she is not rational.

'Mind you, she might well have succeeded where the
others failed. Her idea might have been far more effective.
As you have just said, you are not a man who frightens
easily. The proof is that you are still here in Vallorme.

'But she wanted to do something herself to help the
others. She told us that you were a complex, emotional
and conscientious type who might well have had such
overwhelming feelings of guilt and shame, had she
succeeded—particularly when you found out her real age—
that you would have packed your bag and gone back to
Paris in a hurry.

'Which, of course, was the ultimate object of all the
exercises—to get you away so that you would leave us in
peace. We are quite capable of solving our own problems
here in Vallorme.'

'I see. And this—this—'

Again his hand gestured sweepingly, angrily and even passionately over the table as he remembered—through the pangs of a gnawing and aching hunger—his exquisite meal the night before and thought of what he might have eaten for lunch at that table.

'Oh—that—no—that was my husband's idea. He also wanted to help. If it is any comfort to you, M'sieu Pinaud, may I say that all this has achieved nothing except to make me very unhappy and thoroughly depressed. My pride in my cooking—my reputation—my very self-respect—'

'Of course,' he interjected sympathetically, looking at her for a moment very thoughtfully. Then he continued to speak.

'This business must have been very important to you. To serve such a disgraceful meal must have nearly broken your heart. As you have just said, your own self-respect, madame, your justifiable pride in the magnificence of your cooking— surely you—'

She interrupted him quietly and yet decisively.

'There are so many other things in this life, M'sieu Pinaud, which are so much more important—I am sure I do not have to tell you—than a person's self-respect or pride or self-esteem.'

Then she looked at him directly through the tears that still glistened unshed in her eyes.

'And I can see that everything we have all tried to do is not going to make the slightest difference to what you—'

'None at all,' he interrupted quickly. And then, looking down at her, he smiled suddenly and the hard strong lines of his features were transfigured.

'It would take more than a bad lunch—no—I think this really deserves some stronger term—more than a nightmare meal—to put me off a case. After all—please remember that I am Pinaud of the *Sûreté*. I once went without food for two days while chasing an assassin.

'Mind you, the other ideas were not at all bad—I might well have ended up in hospital, from which I could hardly have continued my investigations. And when I was young—perhaps I should say younger than I am now—that is to say, perhaps after I had just left school, I might easily and enthusiastically—and I know you will be tolerant and forgive me if I add triumphantly—have spent the night with Claudine in your magnificent bed.

'But in the morning—and believe me this is a fact and not conjecture—I would have been back on my investigation. Which is a case of murder, Mme Marceau.'

She met his eyes frankly and a flash of spirit glinted through the unshed tears.

'You are quite wrong, M'sieu Pinaud. We are all agreed here in Vallorme that this was an accident.'

He stood up in one abrupt and even violent movement.

'So I have been given to understand,' he told her quietly. 'Not once but many times. Ever since I arrived in your town of Vallorme. May I tell you here and now, Mme Marceau, that my opinions and my conclusions have not been affected— in spite of so many efforts directed towards that end—in the slightest degree. This information, if you wish, can be divulged freely to all your colleagues, whom you have promised not to name.

'Thank you for being so frank and honest with me, madame—naturally within the limits of your promises—and my gratitude once again for the magnificence of your wonderful cooking last night.'

Without waiting for a reply he walked to the door.

'I will come back to pay my bill later,' he said as he went out.

11

As he drew near, the massive watch-tower seemed to sunder the soft pastel blue of the sky, dark as the distant hills from whence the enemies had always come.

The priest, bareheaded, stood facing him in front of the great carved doors of the church, one of which was slightly open. From the way he stood, M. Pinaud thought again, from the pride and majesty in his bearing, he might well have had a crown on his head and a sword in his hand.

He is expecting me, his thoughts ran on swiftly. He knew that I was coming. Everyone in this town knows what I am doing. And I know nothing.

He bowed his head in reverence and kept his thoughts to himself. Father Lafarge raised his hand and made the sign of the Cross in a silent blessing. When he spoke his words were unexpected.

'Yesterday, M'sieu Pinaud, I listened to you in my garden, because that was your wish. Now whatever you have to say to me, I would like said inside the church. That is my duty and my right.'

He turned and with some difficulty managed to open the door wider.

'As you wish, Father,' M. Pinaud replied quietly.

Inside, the peace and the stillness seemed to reach out to touch him with gentle and compassionate and grieving fingers.

The vast beamed roof soared upwards in a tremendous arch, whose apex was lost in the gloom. The sunlight could not penetrate the windows; the leaded panes were too thick and too small. The candles burned bravely and steadily in the windless air. The statues looked down at them from their niches, part of the peace to which they belonged. The blue and gold figure of the Virgin confronted him with grace and dignity, love and compassion.

M. Pinaud, by nature a reverent man, was acutely conscious of the overwhelming atmosphere of peace and abiding tranquillity. Perhaps because he seldom worshipped in church. To him his God was an intensely personal One, too personal to be shared. For that reason he found it difficult to practise his religion in the company of others, to worship in common.

The priest now turned and faced him. He gestured towards the confessional-box. The resonant voice was muted and quiet, and yet each syllable of every word he said seemed to resound in that all-pervading silence like the tone of the chime of a bell.

'There is something I would like to make clear to you. A penance is not a punishment but an eternal declaration of love for the sinner. The acceptance of the penance by the sinner is another declaration of love—in thankfulness and recognition that the sin, with the help of God, can be expiated.'

There was a long silence, through which M. Pinaud knew that he could still hear the echoes of every word he had uttered.

Suddenly everything was clear and he understood.

'You know, then?' he asked quietly.

'Yes, my son. I know.'

The deep voice vibrated with emotion and feeling.

'I have known since yesterday morning—since the day Colonel Romand met his death. But you know better than to ask me to what I listened in the sacred trust of the confession.'

Again there was a long silence. Then M. Pinaud had one of those typical flashes of insight into human character which was to make him so justifiably famous in the years to come.

'Then it was you—' he began and then stopped.

The priest's eyes, as they met his steadily, were tolerant and wise and understanding.

'Go on, my son,' he said gently.

'It was you who must have organized all these accidents which happened to me. You are the only one I can see capable of planning and co-ordinating such haphazard ideas and getting these so different characters to act together.'

'You are quite right. It was my prerogative and my privilege, and as I saw it, my duty as well.'

He paused for a moment, as if collecting his thoughts and deciding what to say, and then continued.

'I had no fear for your life, M'sieu Pinaud. I have known all these people from the days of their childhood. I baptized and confirmed them, here in this church. I had every confidence in their skill and competence—and not without reason. David Marbon was driving his father's car when he was eleven years old. We all know what Louis Brevin had been able to achieve, by infinite love, patience and understanding, with Nero. That dog is almost human. Ulysse Dumont can fell and lay a tree so that it lands on a pocket-handkerchief. I know—I have seen him do it.

'Besides—and I know you will understand and forgive me when I add what is far more important—both to me and to you—I have been here inside this church on my knees all the time these things were happening—praying for you, that you might be granted wisdom, and humbly beseeching the good God to keep you safely, as you deserve, in His most holy care.'

For the third time there was a silence between them—a silence which to him seemed magnified and hallowed by the brooding peace which sanctified the church.

'A cynic might say that we were wasting our time,' the priest continued. 'But then you are not a cynic, M'sieu Pinaud. Neither am I. Granted we all made a mistake. You are not the man to be swayed or influenced by intimidation. We realize that now—now that it is too late. But no honest effort is ever wasted. We did what we could. And we failed. With another man we might have succeeded. It was worth trying. And you remember the old saying, I am sure—that the failures are those nearest to God.

'We may have failed, but nevertheless we feel proud—

proud that we all tried honestly to achieve something that we believed was right. As proud as you have every right to feel yourself, M'sieu Pinaud, in that your integrity and your courage and your strength of purpose have triumphed over all our efforts to stop you and to drive you away from here.'

'I have my duty, Father,' he replied simply.

'Yes, of course. But to whom?'

'To my employer. To myself and to my conscience. And to my own self-respect.'

'Naturally. But have you thought that there might be a higher duty?'

'To whom?'

'To God.'

'Then I would have been a priest and not a detective.'

The austere and ravaged features in front of him creased into a fleeting and yet charming smile.

'Not necessarily. But you might have made a good one.'

Then the smile disappeared, and the harsh lines of austerity, self-discipline and suffering set his features once again irrevocably into their mould of nobility and pride.

'M'sieu Pinaud—once more I beg you to go. Leave this town alone. Leave us alone. By staying here you can do no good—only infinite harm.'

M. Pinaud shook his head slowly.

'I am thinking of my duty,' he replied quietly.

The priest noticed and wondered at something this man would never have imagined himself—how alike they were, both of them, in their strength, their simplicity and their utter and dedicated conviction.

Then he spoke, very slowly.

'And I am thinking of two things. One is of the English

poet, John Masefield. I once read a poem of his, something about the ship of truth a man can build in which his soul may sail on the sea of death—and how little time he has to do this.

'You remind me very much of that man, M'sieu Pinaud. Because of your fixed conviction that it is only the truth that matters—to you and to everyone else. But what is this thing you have agreed to call truth? Nothing is immutable—that is the whole secret of life. There are laws and principles—causes and effects—that man has not even started to understand in the brief time he has been on this earth. This is surely the greatest truth of all, and one which the wise man should learn to accept.'

His voice changed and softened. Now it was rich and warm with an infinite compassion.

'But that is by the way. I can see that I shall never convince you, M'sieu Pinaud. The other thing is infinitely more important. I am thinking of people—human beings. These people here. My people. People who have suffered and known pain and sorrow, and whose mental anguish and torment have been sometimes almost more than they can bear. People who are still suffering—and still living, M'sieu Pinaud. Not like the one who is dead.'

His eyes closed, and in the few seconds before his lips moved in a silent prayer, it seemed, in the pale and rigid austerity of his features, almost as if one of those stone saints behind them had miraculously exchanged a niche for his cassock . . .

Then his eyes opened and he spoke aloud.

'I am thinking of a man who had to bear the agony of his young daughter taking her own life in shame and despair at what had been done to her. And of a young man who came home from his work to find the sanctuary of his marriage and the happiness of his home defiled and destroyed. Of a man who saw the young girl he loved turned into a nymphomaniac. Of another who gave up a brilliant career only to be near, so that he could help his cousin and her fatherless child. And I am thinking above all of a woman—proud and sensitive and brought up strictly from childhood in a convent—made to suffer unspeakable humiliation and then learn that her own daughter had been defiled and debauched.'

In the silence that he imagined he could almost hear surging softly backwards it seemed then to M. Pinaud that these words spoken aloud had only been a continuation of that silent prayer . . .

After a while he realized with a start that the priest was speaking again.

'These are the people about whom I was thinking, M'sieu Pinaud. The people I consider far more important than your duty. If I have been arrogant I ask you with humility to have the grace to forgive me.'

He shook his head and a faint smile touched and softened the hard and sombre lines of his mouth.

'There is nothing to forgive, Father,' he replied quietly. 'There can be no arrogance in an honest opinion.'

'Thank you. Allow me to ask you a question, M'sieu Pinaud. The innocence of children, I know you will agree, is a sacred trust. What would you think of a man who abused it?'

M. Pinaud shook his head.

'I have no hesitation in answering it, Father. My opinion would almost certainly be exactly the same as yours. But this is not the point at issue. This is not the question. I cannot be concerned with the morals of a man who is dead. I represent the law—'

The interruption came with the rapidity of a swordthrust.

'The law—that is the justice of man. What can the law achieve now? What has it achieved in the past? How can you punish with justice and mercy—what can you do to punish? Take another life—in revenge—in payment of a debt? What punishment is fitting and suitable for a person who already feels remorse and has asked and prayed for a higher forgiveness?'

'One must have law and order—in any community, or else—'

Again the interruption, to his acute and sensitive imagination, seemed to flash in the candlelit gloom with the sharp and gleaming brightness of its utter conviction and sincerity.

'There is law and order in the Kingdom of Heaven, M'sieu Pinaud. Of that there can be no doubt. And there is love and compassion as well—which man has not yet been able to achieve in all his time here on this earth.'

He did not answer. This time the silence no longer surged, but seemed to thrust up like a solid wall between them, separating them, sundering them, dooming them to remain eternally apart . . .

The words, in their bravery and their passionate belief and sublime conviction, seemed to be trying desperately to

191

rise, to surmount and conquer that wall, but they had already been said, and therefore they were dead, since time can never stand still, and he knew that the wall would remain forever between them—if only in proof of the complexity of that creature man, who has not only a body, but the awareness of a soul . . .

He sighed and held out his hand, with dignity and a grace of which he was completely unaware.

'I am sorry, Father,' he said very gently. 'It was the wrong person who asked for forgiveness just now. I ask now for yours, in all humility and with great sincerity. But it seems to me that we both have to walk along different roads.'

The priest's hand was warm and strong and vital.

'God be with you, my son,' he said gravely. 'I shall pray for you, for I believe in my heart that before God you are a man worthy of prayer. But there is only One to Whom a man should pray for forgiveness. You are still a young man— remember that in your life to come. May the grace of God help you and guide you now and give you wisdom and understanding.'

Now he was alone.

Father Lafarge had remained inside the church, in the candlelight and the gloom, but he was walking down the hill in a sunshine that seemed to pour through the dappled autumn leaves of the trees in majestic and liquid shafts of molten gold.

Now he was alone.

And yet not alone, for the words he had heard in that

hallowed and sanctified stillness walked with him, and still resounded through his mind. They seemed to swoop down from beneath the wings of the swallows and house-martins that wheeled and soared above him. They rustled through the swaying branches above the whisper of the wind, and they seemed to glint with gold even as they resounded in his mind . . .

The words were with him, intensely within him, now even part of him, and he knew without the slightest doubt that there they would remain for the rest of his life. The impression they had made was profound.

He came to the bridge and crossed it. He had the strange conviction that he was following his own footsteps, not directing them.

But these words in his mind had been the words of the priest, and not his own. These words had been guiding him to his car and to his home—away from Vallorme with all its sin and its tragedy and its pain.

To vindicate himself he would have to ignore them and believe in his own.

He stopped suddenly and lit a cigarette, if only to break the spell. Then, with a deliberate and conscious effort of will, he directed his steps towards the copse, where it had all begun.

Think of yourself, Pinaud, he reflected as he walked, and not of his words—those splendid, inspiring, compassionate and majestic words that you have just heard. Later you will be able—and proud—to remember them.

But not now. Now you have work to do. You must have faith in yourself that you can do it. You must believe in the ambition that has driven you so far and will carry you even further. You must recognize and admire the pride that always compels you to do that work well.

He turned off up the track opposite the verge where he had changed his wheel and walked rapidly through the shadowed gloom of the copse until he came to the place where he had first seen the body of Colonel Romand.

He recognized the young tree on whose bark he had found traces of the rope, dropped to his knees beside it and began to search again, slowly and carefully and methodically.

He had no idea for what he was searching. He did not even know if he would find anything. But he knew, with a complete and dominant conviction, that for the sake of his own self-respect, he had to try.

He turned over leaves and twigs and branches, he tore his skin and flesh on thorns and brambles, he winced at the pain of nettles, and he dug his fingers and tore his nails fruitlessly under tangled and protruding roots.

And still he found nothing.

The marks and abrasions of the rope or cord were still on the bark of the tree, and that was all. His nails and fingers were dark with mud and slime and mould from rotting leaves. The once immaculate bandage of Dr Justeron looked as if it had been taken from a dustbin.

But still he would not give up.

He went on searching, extending his operations into ever widening circles about the base of the tree. On a thick bush just behind it he found a branch that had been cracked and split. The wood was green and not dead. It could not have been the wind, since there was the shelter of other bushes and shrubs all around. Someone had pressed too close to its dense foliage for concealment.

Disjointed ideas and memories raced through his mind

in the instantaneous wonder of thought. The fact that he had not found anything did not mean that there was nothing to find, only that he had not searched in the right place.

He remembered once again his headmaster at school. Genius, Pinaud, is nothing more than an infinite capacity for taking pains. He remembered something else he had once been told when he was very young—if a thing is worth doing it is worth doing well. But all the time he went on searching he was conscious of a vague regret that he could not recall who had told him that.

Then, at last, turning over a mass of newly fallen leaves, he found a small white ivory ring.

12

He let the knocker fall slowly and heavily on the white panelled door.

She opened it quickly and looked at him, dully and apathetically, almost as if trying to remember who he might be.

For his part, he looked at her with a new interest.

Here was a woman who no longer cared what she wore. Her clothes, from their appearance, had probably been taken off the night before, flung over the back of a chair and put on again this morning without heed or care or attention. She wore the same blue linen dress, now rumpled and creased, and the same belt with the white ivory rings.

Bravely she forced a smile to her lined and suffering features.

'M'sieu Pinaud—how kind of you to call—'

He looked at her directly, wordlessly, and his eyes were

neither stern nor accusing, but soft and dark with a great compassion.

He held out the ivory ring he had found towards her on the palm of his hand, as she saw it the words died before they reached her mouth, strangled by the constriction in her throat.

'I should think that this one must have dropped from your belt yesterday,' he said quietly, 'while you were tightening the rope round the tree.'

There was a long silence, in which it seemed to him that she and the whole world and perhaps he himself too, had all stopped breathing.

She looked steadily into his eyes for what seemed to him to be an interminable time, and then, as if making a decision, she slowly inclined her head. She reached out and took the ring from his hand. Then she stepped back and opened the door wide.

'You had better come inside, M'sieu Pinaud,' she said. Her voice was so quiet—softer than the rustle of the falling leaves outside—that he hardly heard it.

She ushered him into the living-room and then turned to face him with a sudden and disarming smile.

'I think it would be better,' she continued in that same quiet voice, 'if we both had a glass of wine together. It will help to make things so much easier—for you to listen and especially for me to talk to you. Please excuse me while I fetch the bottle.'

'Thank you, madame,' he replied. 'I am inclined to agree with you.'

She left him alone. He stood there waiting beside a chair, rigid and tense, until she returned with two bottles and two large glasses on a tray. She placed it carefully on a small table.

'Do please sit down, M'sieu Pinaud,' she said in her normal voice. 'It is my turn to pour.'

Again she tried to smile. A sudden rush of emotion at her courage for a second made him catch his breath even as it dimmed his eyes. He sat down and tried desperately to relax.

She poured the wine and handed him his glass. Then she took hers and sat down in a high chair opposite him.

She raised her glass.

'I told you last night that there were no longer any toasts in this unhappy house,' she said. 'But I was wrong. I drink to you, M'sieu Pinaud—as a token of appreciation for all your kindness, tolerance and courtesy to us who live in it. Your very good health.'

He tried but could not speak. He lifted his glass and drained its contents in one gigantic swallow.

For the third and last time, as she began to get up, she tried to smile. He held up his hand fiercely and was out of his chair in a second, turning his head away so that she would not see the tears in his eyes.

He filled his glass to the brim, lifted and drained it. The wine—perhaps because of what he had drunk for lunch—seemed even more incredibly exquisite than the night before. He filled the glass again and took two more mouthfuls, very slowly. And all the time he kept his back to her.

When he turned she was holding out her empty glass, without looking at him. She was intently watching the house-martins as they swooped and wheeled with fantastic grace and speed to and from their nests under the eaves.

He took the glass from her hand and went back to the tray, where he refilled it, still keeping his back turned. Then he saw that there was not very much left in his own glass, so he emptied and refilled it. By now the first bottle was looking somewhat the worse for wear.

Then he went back to his chair, handed her the glass and sat down.

'Thank you,' she said. Then she continued without a pause. 'Only those who never drink do not realize what a comfort and a blessing wine can be as it dulls the sharp edge of pain.'

She drank a little and then placed her glass down carefully on the carpet.

'I said that I would tell you about Claudine,' she began. 'But to tell you in a way that you will understand I must first start by telling you about myself. She is my daughter— my own flesh and blood.'

'I was brought up by an invalid mother and two dominant spinster aunts. They looked after her as well, devotedly and efficiently. As I grew older her health grew worse. The decision was taken that I should be sent to a convent school as a boarding pupil, which would obviously lighten their burden and at the same time be of inestimable benefit to me.'

She paused for a moment and made a sound that might have been a short sharp laugh, only in it there was nothing of mirth.

'At least the Sisters of the Holy Order of St Augustine

taught me grace and dignity, which are so sadly lacking in this world today.

'Apart from that, they taught me nothing—except to be thoroughly and decently ashamed of my body and my perfectly normal and healthy sexual desires. We were compelled to keep on a vest when we took a bath—believe it or not. The human body was something vaguely indecent and sinful.

'I knew nothing of life, therefore, when I was married. The good Sisters, in their fanatical devotion to a celibate and dedicated life, had assured me not once but many times, that the only way to inner peace was to join their Order and become one of them.

'If I were obstinate enough to insist on getting married, they continued, then certain extremely unpleasant and even unhygienic things were bound to happen to me. The only thing to do—since they would be inevitable—would be to shut my eyes tightly and pray that the whole humiliating, disgusting and degrading business would soon be over.

'Mercifully, I married an understanding, gentle and sensitive man. On my wedding night I was quite prepared to shut my eyes as I had been advised, and to pray for strength and courage to endure him.

'But there was no need. We loved each other and together we found a great and wonderful happiness—an exaltation that I had never dreamed could exist.'

She paused for a moment and closed her eyes. He waited in silence, with tact, sympathy and understanding, while she re-lived in her mind, briefly and thankfully, those memories that had been such happy ones.

Then she opened her eyes and shivered. She picked up

her glass, drank the wine, glanced at his empty one, and held her own out to him.

'Please open the other bottle, M'sieu Pinaud—the corkscrew is on the tray.'

'Thank you, madame,' he replied quietly as he stood up and took the glass from her outstretched hand.

The silence lasted until he came back to his chair. She thanked him, drank a little, and then continued to speak, her face grave and composed.

'I find this wine a very great help. To talk to you like this—so intimately—is not easy for me, as you can well imagine, but I have told you all these things deliberately so that you may be able to understand Claudine better.

'I love her more than anything in this world. What I have done—I did for her. She is my daughter. She has my own nature. She is part of me—the finer part of me. All that was repressed in me by those fanatical Sisters was encouraged, sanely and rationally, and allowed to develop, naturally and beautifully and joyfully—as it should have been—by me, her mother, with the help of the kindest and most considerate of husbands.

'With the result that she grew to the threshold of womanhood with a beautiful body, of which she was justly and joyfully proud.'

Again she paused and drank some wine. Again he waited in silence.

There were so many things he could say—that he wanted to say—that he felt he ought to say, but he knew as well that this was not the time to say them.

This woman had more to say than he would ever have. The silence was hers by right.

'And then her father died. To me it was as if the whole

world had ended. Mercifully, I still had Claudine. I was forced to think of her. My own personal grief and sorrow— for my own sanity and good—seemed unimportant when compared to her future. My husband had left very little money. I would have been compelled to sell this house.

'Then Colonel Romand came to Vallorme when he retired from the Army. I was introduced to him and very impressed by his personality and charm, of which he had plenty.

'There were tales already going around the town that he had been asked to resign because of some scandal, but I ignored them. I was already thinking of Claudine and her future. I felt that I owed it to her to put my personal feelings to one side and do whatever was necessary to safeguard her future. He was a wealthy man. He was looking for a house in Vallorme, the birthplace of his ancestors. Claudine would be able to continue to live here, in this house she had grown to love as her home.'

She hesitated and looked around the room as if seeing it for the first time. 'Naturally I had misgivings, feelings of panic, emotions and doubts. But I forced myself, quite deliberately and ruthlessly, to suppress them all. Whatever I felt, whatever apprehensions I may have had—what could be their importance compared to the future happiness of my daughter?

'I felt supremely confident of myself. If I—in spite of a convent upbringing—could once make a success of that tragic and degrading ordeal they considered a marriage, then surely— for the sake of my own daughter—I could do it again.

'Even if all the rumours and stories about him were

true—which was unlikely, since gossip is usually malicious—
I had every confidence in myself to be able to influence
and guide him to live a happy and contented life.'

She sighed and closed her eyes for a moment. He
waited. This was not the time to interrupt.

'If only I had known. If only I had thought—with my
head instead of my heart. But all my thoughts were only of
my daughter Claudine, and what I could do to give her
happiness and the future she deserved.

'I should have known. I should have guessed. When I
looked down at his dead face yesterday morning I could
see so clearly on every feature the evil that had destroyed
his soul.

'But when he was eager and smiling, and gracious and
understanding, he seemed to be a different man. Or perhaps it was all my fault. Perhaps I was so desperately
wanting to see a different man that I imagined one—a
husband I was only too willing to accept and tolerate,
provided he would give Claudine a home.'

She paused for a moment and once again there was
silence. He did not speak. He could not speak. His thoughts
were confused and chaotic, terrifying and sad.

She reached for her glass and emptied it in one quick
and somehow almost desperate swallow. He hastened to
rise from his chair, took it with his own and refilled them
both at the tray—automatically, hardly aware of what he
was doing, trying vainly to sort out and understand the
thoughts that were racing in such mad confusion through
his mind . . .

'Thank you,' she said. And then without a pause she
continued to speak.

'I could take off this dress now and show you the bruises and the burns and the weals on my skin—his way of stopping me from going to Father Lafarge—if it is possible that you do not believe me—if you should still have doubts as to—'

He held up his hand and interrupted her.

'I believe you, madame.'

'Thank you. When I found out that he had debauched his own stepdaughter and aroused her erotically long before she was really ready for it—with the results that you have seen yourself—I knew what had to be done. Yesterday morning I did it. For Claudine's sake.'

The slow tortured voice ceased.

He sat perfectly still and did not speak—so still and silent that it seemed he had almost become a part of the ensuing silence. This he did deliberately.

This was a silence that he knew—intuitively, instinctively and certainly—that she must find soothing and healing—a silence that seemed to surge in benediction to accept and enfold and engulf all the pain and the humiliation and the shame that seemed to quiver, like the broken wings of a bird, over each dreadful word she had forced herself to say.

This silence she would welcome. In it lay the anodyne and the relief and the assuagement for the horror she had been compelled to tell . . .

* * *

Abruptly and quickly she stood up, facing him. Her head was held high and proud, but he saw her lips quiver and a muscle twitch beneath her eye, and he could sense the tense emotion that was drawing her quivering nerves taut with anxiety and fear.

'Now that you have heard all this—now that you know the truth—what are you going to do?'

He stood up as well, but with deliberation and no haste. His movements were lithe, smooth and coordinated, and imbued with an unconscious grace by his exceptional physical strength. Because of this, he did not spill a drop from the brimming glass he held in his hand.

He looked down at it gravely and then moved to the small table with the tray. Standing there with his back to her, he lifted the glass and emptied it in one long smooth swallow.

Then he turned and came back to face her. He looked directly into her eyes and smiled, and the hard strong lines of his features were transfigured.

'Nothing,' he told her quietly.

'What do you mean?'

'I mean what I say. You asked what I was going to do. The answer is nothing.'

'I—I do not understand—'

'It was an accident—as several of the inhabitants of Vallorme have been at some considerable pains to tell me. I suggest you put that ivory ring back on your belt as soon as I have left. That is the only evidence there is. Since there is no other, the inhabitants of Vallorme are obviously right and I was wrong.'

'But you know now it was not—'

'You did what you thought right,' he interrupted her gently. 'Listen, madame—you have sinned and suffered, repented and confessed, and Father Lafarge has given you absolution. That is all there is to it. Whatever I think or say can be of no importance.'

For a long moment she stared at him incredulously, and then the tears came, sudden and blinding, healing and merciful. The proud head bowed and she raised her hands to cover her face in a gesture he found infinitely and intolerably pathetic.

Instinctively, generously, he took one swift step forward and took her in his arms. He felt her wince and shudder as his hard muscles hurt the tender and bruised flesh beneath her dress, and he reached up one hand to smooth back the hair from her brow in a gesture of infinite gentleness and compassion.

Suddenly all his own ambitions, his dedication and loyalty to his work, his pride in his own achievements—all seemed very small and insignificant beside the suffering and the sorrow this unhappy woman had been compelled to endure.

For a fleeting moment, as they stood there together, premonition seemed to come to touch him with the same gentle, grieving and compassionate embrace with which he was trying to comfort this sad and tormented woman in his arms.

Premonition seemed to use that same pity and understanding he had given her so spontaneously and so generously— now trying to warn him of what was to come.

Premonition and a sense of doom were in some indefinable way both there together—until it was as if he could sense and anticipate all the terror of the unknown, the pain and the guilt and the remorse, the violence and the bloodshed, the danger and the horror of the hair-raising escapes from death, the fear and the terror and torment—all that was destined to comprise his own life during the long and dangerous years to come. He closed his eyes and shivered at the pity and the tragedy and the inevitability of it all . . .

Then he opened them, lowered his hands and his arms, and looked down at her.

The scene in the church was as vivid in his mind as if it had happened seconds ago.

The words of the priest, his blessing, his kindness and tolerance, and his prayers for him had made a profound and lasting impression.

He knew now—since that incredible premonition had told him—something of what he would have to face in his life to come.

Because of his very nature, he faced it unafraid. But he knew as well, with a humility as rare as it was commendable, that he did not dare to face it alone . . .

He needed help. He would need help, as he had been granted the mercy of help and protection here in this strange town of Vallorme. He was not ashamed to ask for it. Without that help he was and throughout his life would be nothing.

'Would you be kind enough,' he said quietly, 'to do something for me, Mme Romand?'

She looked up at him, her eyes still swollen with tears but shining now with a great and wonderful peace.

'Of course. You have only to ask. To you I owe everything. I can find no words to express my gratitude—'

'The way you live will be your gratitude,' he interrupted her suddenly. And although his voice was gentle and quiet there was a conviction, a respect and an encouragement in his words that she knew would give her the strength to fulfill them. 'But when you go next to church, would you please light a candle for me.'

Then he turned away, walked to the door, opened it and left her alone.